Extortion & Enmity: A Pride & Prejudice Variation Mystery Romance

Crime & Courtship, Volume 3

Abbey North

Published by Abbey North JAFF Books, 2022.

EXTORTION & ENMITY: A PRIDE & PREJUDICE VARIATION MYSTERY ROMANCE

First edition. February 10, 2022.

Copyright © 2022 Abbey North.

ISBN: 979-8215449677

Written by Abbey North.

Blurb

Lizzy arrives at Hunsford to visit Charlotte, having mixed feelings to discover Darcy is in the vicinity to see his aunt, the formidable Lady Catherine. They are inevitably thrown together, and she starts to see a different side to him. When Miss Anne becomes the victim of an extortion scheme, Lizzy volunteers to help identify the blackmailer. She is surprised when Mr. Darcy volunteers his assistance, seemingly accepting the situation and his cousin's actions. It leads to a new accord between them, but with Darcy unchanged, how can she even consider, let alone accept, an unexpected proposition after they find the extortionist?

This is part three of the "Crime & Courtship" series, which will be five books, intended to be read in order, and follow roughly the same timeline and location as J.A.'s masterpiece. The first mystery takes place in Meryton. The next will be at Netherfield, followed by Hunsford, then London, and finally Pemberley. The story arc will continue throughout all five parts, compromising one long read broken into five sections. A mystery is central to each installment, so you could call this a cozy mystery sweet Regency romance.

While Abbey sometimes writes sensual JAFF, this series is strictly SWEET.

Chapter One

The trip to Hunsford passed without remarkability, and Lizzy and Maria Lucas arrived that afternoon. It was several days past the events at Netherfield, and her sister Jane was already on her way to London, the process hastened by Fanny insisting she take the carriage once her mother had learned why Jane wanted to go to London early. She was hardly surprised by that, indeed thinking her mother would have carried Jane on her back herself if it meant getting her closer to Mr. Bingley and the possibility of matrimony.

The Lucas' carriage, which Lord Lucas had offered upon learning Jane was using the other one and Maria wanted to visit as well, drew up outside the Hunsford Rectory, and Lizzy saw Charlotte waiting for her. Mr. Collins stood slightly behind her, and a small shudder went through her as it did each time she saw him after a separation.

She couldn't help remembering his unwelcome proposal, hardly waiting to give her a chance to say yes or no before he started laying out the details of their life together. It had been a nasty confrontation when she'd spoken up harshly and told him she would never marry him. Though three years in the past, each time she saw him after long absences, it was immediately at the forefront of her mind.

As he greeted her stiffly moments later, she couldn't help thinking it was the same for Mr. Collins. No doubt, he recalled his humiliation at her hands each time they met again, but inevitably, they would both adapt in the next few days and manage a modicum of civility.

They both did it for Charlotte, and she was relieved to see Mr. Collins seemed to genuinely adore his wife, though she wasn't as confident of Charlotte's feelings. Charlotte seemed quite content though, especially with her burgeoning belly, and Lizzy couldn't help reaching out a hand to touch it. "Congratulations, Lottie."

"Thank you, Eliza," said Charlotte as she hugged her. "We are quite excited."

"Indeed, for what man does not look forward to expanding his family? Indeed, I was just telling Lady de Bourgh the other day that—"

Lizzy allowed Mr. Collins's meandering words to flow over her, giving a polite nod every few moments as he pontificated about the subject for far longer than was necessary. It was long enough to take them into the house, provide a refresher for how everything was arranged, though Lizzy hadn't forgotten in the six months since her last visit, and instill her in a room.

Mr. Collins was still discussing the topic when Charlotte gently shut the door in his face and followed her into the room, hugging her again. "I have missed you, Eliza. How are you?"

Lizzy sighed as she sat down on the bed. "That is a complicated question, my dear. I fear we shall need at least two pots of tea to make sense of everything that has happened."

Charlotte's lips twitched. "In that case, I shall order them immediately. Mr. Collins will eventually lose the passion for his current topic and wander off." She sounded indulgent.

Lizzy's looked at her closely. "Are you happy, Lottie?"

Charlotte's eyes widened. "Of course, Lizzy. I am most practical, and marriage has been exactly as I anticipated. Though I did not enter the union with starry eyes and the expectation of deep love, Mr. Collins does grow on one, and I find our marriage quite tolerable."

"I am happy for you." Lizzy struggled not to betray any hint of sadness for her friend. It seemed to her that marriage should be much more than tolerable, but she also understood Charlotte had been left on the shelf for too long and was prepared to take a less-than-satisfying union by the time Mr. Collins had proposed to her. At that point, she had been four-and-twenty and already deemed a spinster by all those around her. Unlike Lizzy, Charlotte had not been amenable to that thought.

They left her room a short time later, finding Maria in the hallway, looking practically trapped as Mr. Collins told her in excruciating detail the difficulty of keeping the roses Lady Catherine's gardener had provided clippings of alive in the persnickety soil of the garden bed he'd chosen. Maria seemed relieved to see them, and Lizzy could hardly blame her.

The four of them adjourned to Charlotte's sitting room, and Lizzy knew from previous visits that Mr. Collins rarely intruded there. He sat down to join them for a cup of tea, and he dominated the conversation, as they all expected. She was relieved when he realized the lateness of the hour and declared he must work on the Sunday sermon.

He paused to look at Maria and Lizzy, beaming at them. "We have a special treat, my dears. Lady de Bourgh has invited us for dinner tomorrow evening, and I am certain you are swooning at the opportunity. It is what can only be the highlight of your visit for the times we are condescended by Lady de Bourgh to be allowed in her presence."

"Indeed, it is one of the main reasons I come to visit," said Lizzy with complete seriousness. Since Charlotte wasn't facing her husband, she was free to grin like mad, which made it difficult for Lizzy to maintain her solemn expression.

Apparently, Mr. Collins didn't pick up any sarcasm, for he nodded in an enthusiastic fashion. "Indeed, indeed. She is the most benevolent patroness. Did I tell you what she has done for us of late? Why just last week, she was having her fences whitewashed, and she sent her crew over to do ours as well."

"Most generous," said Maria in a soft voice. Her lips were trembling, and Lizzy imagined she was having a difficult time not laughing either. She didn't know Maria nearly as well as she knew

Charlotte, for the sisters were a good ten years apart in age, and this was Maria's first trip alone to visit her sister, save with Lizzy, but she was happy to see Maria might share a similar sense of humor to Charlotte.

Before he could start pontificating yet again, Charlotte cleared her throat. "My dear, your sermon will not write itself."

He put a hand on her shoulder, patting gently. "Of course. You do keep me on track, my dear." He bent to press a kiss to Charlotte's cheek, and then he stood. "I shall see you ladies at dinner, and of course, we can discuss more about Lady de Bourgh then."

"There are no words to describe how much I look forward to that," said Lizzy with what she hoped was passable sincerity.

For just a moment, Mr. Collins blinked, as though he was on the edge of realizing she was mocking him slightly, but then the expression flitted away, and he beamed at her. "Indeed. It is a topic of which I never tire."

"I can certainly vouch for that," said Maria. "Upon my last visit, I do declare Lady de Bourgh was the most dominant topic of conversation." She sounded almost admiring of that, but her twinkling eyes gave her away.

Mr. Collins nodded at her in a benevolent fashion. "Quite right. My dear, Sister Maria, and Cousin Eliza, I shall see you all at dinner."

Finally, he departed. They waited for a moment, and Lizzy wondered if the two sisters were also holding off discussing anything more important while they paused to see if Mr. Collins would actually depart, or if he would return with yet another insightful statement about his patroness.

When it seemed like he was gone for now, Charlotte refreshed their teacups and leaned back. "Do tell me everything, Eliza."

"It is quite a long and involved tale." She shot a glance at Maria, who was just now coming out into society, so she wasn't perhaps familiar with everything that had occurred. "We had a thief in Meryton."

"Miss Eliza was instrumental in discovering the identity," said Maria. "Mr. Darcy helped, did he not, Miss Eliza?"

She nodded as Charlotte's interest piqued. "Who is this Mr. Darcy? Do you have a beau, Lizzy?"

Before she could cull the impulse, Lizzy snorted. "I would rather be courted by a donkey in a bonnet than by Mr. Fitzwilliam Darcy. Indeed, both are asses, but I fear the prospect of spending time with Darcy over the donkey would be more unendurable."

Charlotte's lips twitched. "He sounds most unpleasant indeed. You must tell me about him."

"He is tall and handsome, with dark hair and dark eyes. He has an income of ten thousand per year, and he must most assuredly be in want of a wife, at least according to common gossip." Lizzy sipped her tea, noting the quality. "This is an excellent blend."

Charlotte nodded. "Mr. Collins has ordered a pleasing selection from India of late. I believe it is because I crave cardamom so heavily, and it is frightfully expensive." She rubbed her stomach in an indulgent fashion. "Perhaps he or she is the one craving cardamom."

"It is superb."

"So, the gentleman is handsome and rich, and yet you would prefer to be wooed by a donkey in a bonnet? He must have something dreadfully wrong with him," said Charlotte.

"He is most insulting," said Maria. She sipped her tea before adding, "He gave great offense at the Assembly ball, and though he was helpful in discovering Wickham was the thief, people generally hold him in low opinion in Meryton."

"It is true," said Lizzy. "He did make a deplorable impression upon all, but when his sister was abducted at the Netherfield ball, I was pleased to see how many of our townspeople rallied around him and offered to help find her."

Charlotte's eyes widened. "A kidnapping after the thefts? Oh, my. I see what you mean about needing two pots of tea." She rang the bell beside her, and the housekeeper appeared moments later. "Mrs. Tesch, would you please ensure we have a new pot of tea and more of those delicious raspberry cakes?"

"Of course, Mrs. Collins," said the woman with a bow before she disappeared once more.

"Miss Eliza helped find his sister too. She is quite the hero of Meryton."

Lizzy's cheeks flushed as she pondered whether to share with Maria how much she disliked the diminutive Eliza. Realizing Maria and Mr. Collins would both take their cues from Charlotte's usage of the nickname, she decided not to bother. "I assure you, it was not by design. I had merely stumbled across Wickham's hideout earlier in the day, and he had stayed close to it when he took Miss Georgiana."

Charlotte stiffened suddenly. "Did you say Fitzwilliam Darcy and Georgiana Darcy?"

Lizzy nodded. "Indeed. Why?"

Charlotte smiled. "I do know the gentleman in question, and his kind sister. Mr. Darcy visits Lady Catherine at least twice a year, and Georgiana has been an infrequent visitor along with him." She frowned, appearing trapped in consternation. "The very same Mr. Darcy was the one who helped to solve the mystery and retrieve his sister? I can hardly credit the idea. The man is so reserved and prideful. I do not believe I have spoken more than a dozen words to him in the three years of my marriage."

"That does sound like Fitzwilliam Darcy. You can see how unbelievable it was that he and I managed to work together to identify a thief, and then to find Miss Georgiana."

Charlotte's lips lifted into a smile. "I believe I might see why you would prefer a donkey in a bonnet, dear Eliza." The three ladies giggled at that, and then conversation switched to something else.

Lizzy felt relaxed and better than she had in a while to be in the presence of her dear friend, though she wished the image of Mr. Darcy would stop plaguing her. Even when she thought she was thinking about something else, his face would surge into her mind, or she would recall a snippet of conversation, or perhaps an ugly moment when they had exchanged acrimonious words on more than one occasion. It was as though the man was haunting her, and she was ready to exorcise him permanently.

THE FOLLOWING EVENING could not be delayed or put off, but Lizzy had hoped for some sort of calamity to prevent it. She had been a reluctant guest at Rosings Park for dinner many times, but she'd never looked forward to it. Lady de Bourgh was condescension itself, along with being full of strong opinions one did not dare go against. The few times Lizzy had voiced an opposite opinion, she had been thoroughly chastised for the ignorance of youth and the failure to see Lady de Bourgh's wisdom.

Dinner there was exhausting, but at least there was a bright spot. She did look forward to seeing Miss Anne, Lady Catherine's daughter. The other woman was a few years older than Lizzy, and she was generally regarded as a spinster due to her ill-health. She didn't speak much, but when she did, Lizzy usually found her words insightful, and the woman had a calm presence about her that invited others to be restful too. The only people who seemed impervious to that were her mother and Mr. Collins.

They had visited for a while in the salon before coming through to the dining room when the butler announced it was time for dinner, and now Lizzy found herself seated across from Maria and beside Charlotte, with Anne on her other side. Lady de Bourgh was at the head of the table, and Mr. Collins sat beside Charlotte. There were several chairs that remained unused, since the dining table was exquisitely long.

"Tell me about your life, Miss Bennet," said Lady de Bourgh.

Lizzy clenched her teeth, having had this conversation at least once per visit. She couldn't be certain if Lady Catherine simply couldn't be bothered to remember any details about her, or if it were a means of reminding her how inconsequential she was.

She briefly considered changing the tale of her life, wondering if she could scandalize Lady Catherine by implying her parents were circus performers, and she had a sister with four arms, but she decided against it, though the amusement allowed her to flash Lady Catherine a brighter smile than she could've otherwise. "There is little to tell, Lady Catherine. I come from a humble family, and we have five daughters altogether, but no sons."

"How distressing for your poor father. Who will inherit your property?"

"Mr. Collins," said Lizzy too-sweetly. "The entailment dictates the property must go to the next male heir. I am certain you are familiar with such arrangements." She struggled not to sound bitter that neither she nor her sisters could be deemed worthy of inheriting Longbourn, with or without a husband.

She understood the advisability of not splitting up an estate among multiple siblings, but she saw no good reason why Jane couldn't be the one to inherit Longbourn, since she was the eldest child. It shouldn't matter if she were a woman, or if she were unmarried. That was the way of society though, and there was little Lizzy could do to change it.

"Oh, that is the property you expect to inherit someday, Mr. Collins. Very good." Lady de Bourgh looked at her rector with a fond smile. "I know you must long for that day."

Lizzy clenched her teeth again, wanting to call Lady Catherine on her insensitivity, but she knew there was no point. The woman was either deliberately insulting, or obliviously insensitive. That was almost worse than the first.

"Indeed, it will be quite a splendid day when we take Longbourn. I have many plans for it, you see." Mr. Collins started to launch into them, but Charlotte cleared her throat.

"It will be a challenging time for Eliza's family when that happens, Mr. Collins," she said with a repressive note in her voice. "Perhaps we should discuss something less upsetting."

"Nonsense," said Lady Catherine. "I am certain Miss Bennet is up to the conversation. After all, it must linger in her thoughts a great deal that her circumstances will change beyond recognition once her father dies." Lady de Bourgh turned her gaze on Lizzy again. "Tell me, dear, have any of your sisters made smart matches?"

Lizzy clamped her lips together for a moment, trying to draw a deep breath to keep from blurting out something rude. "We are all young, and Papa is in good health, so I confess it is not a thought on many of our minds." She didn't bother to mention her mother's obsession with the thought, for indeed, though she occasionally mocked her mother and was certainly embarrassed by her behavior, she refused to expose her to gossip or cutting comments from someone like Lady Catherine.

"Such a lackadaisical attitude to take toward the matter. If I were you, young lady, I would focus on getting a beau and turning him into a husband quickly. You never know how fate may change from one day to the next. After all, my dear Lewis died unexpectedly, and your dear papa might do the same at any moment."

Lizzy wished she could be surprised by the other woman's callousness, but after similar meetings in the past, there was little Catherine could do to shock her. She just nodded and allowed the woman to drone on about the importance of estate planning, a good marriage, and what Mr. Collins would do to Longbourn.

Apparently, Anne was satisfied her mother would continue to speak for a while, so she leaned over and squeezed Lizzy's hand under the table briefly. "I am sorry for my mother. She can be dreadfully awful sometimes."

Lizzy grinned at her, keeping her voice low as well. "You have my sympathy, and my complete understanding, for my mother can be quite dreadful as well." Though when contrasted with Lady Catherine, Fanny seemed little more than a slight annoyance upon occasion.

She had much to recommend her over the other woman, including genuine warmth and affection for her daughters, though Lizzy often felt like Fanny didn't understand her and vice versa. She still knew her mother loved her, even if she was perplexed by her very existence.

Dinner finally ended, and Lizzy had engaged in more conversation with Anne in a discreet fashion, since it wouldn't do to be singled out for not listening to Lady Catherine or Mr. Collins. It was difficult to determine who was more long-winded, though Lady Catherine had the singular ability to be able to quiet Mr. Collins with a word or a look.

Indeed, it was quite amusing to see him stop in the middle of a thought when the lady indicated it was time for her to speak, or she just blurted out whatever she was thinking, uncaring who was speaking before her. To Lizzy, she had dreadful manners, especially considering her station in life, and she was quite surprised to learn Mr. Darcy was related to the woman. It proved to her that extreme wealth and every advantage couldn't make one a decent person.

As Mr. Collins was the only one in attendance, there was no need for him to dismiss himself with the other men for a glass of port or a cigar after dinner, and Lizzy couldn't imagine him partaking in such extravagances anyway. Instead, they endured another round of tea and more conversation before they were finally freed.

"It is getting late, and you must return to the rectory before it gets too dark, but I wish for you to come back for dinner in two days, Mr. Collins. You shall be delighted to know my nephews are soon visiting. Richard and Fitzwilliam will be here tomorrow, and I will wish to greet them with a proper family dinner tomorrow evening, but they will be ready to entertain the day after. I have no doubt it will be refreshing for your guests to experience the company of two such fine gentlemen."

Lizzy barely hid a grimace at the news. After all, what were the odds Lady de Bourgh had two nephews named Fitzwilliam? Still, she made herself ask, "Would that be Fitzwilliam Darcy, Lady de Bourgh?"

Catherine looked at her, frowning. "Yes. What would you know of my nephew?"

Lizzy managed a bland smile. "Not much. He recently stayed at Netherfield with his friend, Mr. Bingley. I met him a few times."

Catherine's nose wrinkled. "The Bingleys," she said with a hint of distaste in her tone. "Tradesmen, the lot of them. In my day, no Fitzwilliam would have associated with one such as them, but I realize things have changed. Those of us with higher standing must necessarily compromise upon occasion as the standards of society yield to those who can afford to pave the way for the lessening."

Lizzy clenched her hands in her lap, wishing to defend Mr. Bingley, but knowing she had no right to. She certainly wasn't about to explain to Lady Catherine why she felt semi-protective of the young man her sister loved so fervently.

She was surprised to find Darcy wasn't quite as pretentious as his aunt, because he didn't seem to let it bother him that Mr. Bingley's money came from trade. Indeed, if Mr. Darcy could retain a friend, he appeared to in Charles Bingley, and she couldn't imagine many people being able to dislike the young man. She wondered if Lady Catherine had even met him, or if she had simply passed judgment on him because of his familial origins.

She also couldn't help thinking about the lady's hypocrisy as the party returned to Hunsford. Lady Catherine herself was inviting social inferiors for dinner and entertaining them, though they were more a captive audience to Lizzy's way of thinking.

She was bemoaning that her nephew would interact with a tradesman who made four thousand per year, while she was hosting her vicar and his wife. Lizzy wondered if she'd given any thought to the situation, and how she reconciled her beliefs with her actions, but she doubted Lady Catherine was a deep enough thinker to have ever realized she behaved in a contrary fashion to her espoused beliefs.

As she was getting into bed later, she realized she had successfully distracted herself from thinking about her forthcoming meeting with Darcy. Now, lying in bed alone, there was nothing else she could force her thoughts to focus on, and she realized she was looking forward to the prospect in a way she hadn't expected.

Of course, part it would be the pleasure of needling Darcy if she got the chance, and she would most certainly be sure to ask after Mr. Bingley. Of course, she genuinely wanted to know if Georgiana was all right after her abduction, but she shouldn't be looking forward to seeing him.

She took herself to task for the idea, recalling the many reasons why she should be dreading the meeting entirely. For one, he was determined to keep Bingley apart from Jane, and he had called Jane a grasping social climber. That was the farthest thing from the truth, for her sister was kindness and compassion itself. She would've loved Mr. Bingley if he had been a goatherder instead of having wealth from a familial history of trade.

Besides, Mr. Darcy seemed on the verge of announcing his engagement to Miss Caroline Bingley, Charles's sister. She had no business feeling any kind of excitement to see someone else's betrothed, though the announcement had not yet been formally given the last she'd heard. She knew it was coming, implied by Darcy himself, so why would she be excited to see him?

She was grudgingly forced to admit she found Mr. Darcy attractive. Who wouldn't, as long as a woman had eyes? He was a handsome man, and he cut a fine figure. If it hadn't been for his horrible manner and contemptuous disposition, he would've been a true Incomparable, and any woman would have fallen for him.

Not that she had fallen for him, Lizzy hastily assured herself. Sharing an investigation into the thefts, and then a dramatic rescue of his sister from her kidnapping, was hardly a basis to build a relationship, especially with a man like him. Physical attraction was quite separate from emotional accord, and that was something she was certain they would never find. They could have years to do so and still fail, for she couldn't imagine they would ever be able to get along in a civilized fashion for long.

She firmly squashed any sense of enthusiasm at the idea of seeing him, reminding herself how inappropriate it was, and just how boorish the man could be. He looked down on everything and everyone, and that most certainly encompassed a country miss like Elizabeth Bennet.

Chapter Two

Fitzwilliam had been bracing himself all day for this, ever since learning the day before that Elizabeth Bennet was a guest at Hunsford, and she would be coming for dinner this evening. The last place he'd expected to see her—and truthfully, he'd never expected to see her again—had been in his aunt's parlor at Rosings Park.

That the lady could entertain Elizabeth Bennet seemed laughable, but he knew she tended to invite the Collins couple multiple times per week. He suspected she enjoyed having someone listen to her speak, and normally, he was quite tolerant of sharing that duty with others. It was only that Elizabeth Bennet was part of the party that bothered him, though he strove not to show it as they entered the sitting room to visit before dinner.

She didn't look at him at all, and in fact, she seemed to be studiously looking anywhere but his direction. Feeling annoyed at that, he walked forward, taking time to greet Mrs. Collins and meet Maria Lucas, who looked vaguely familiar. He thought he might've seen her during his short stay at Netherfield, but he couldn't be certain. He turned to Lizzy last. "Miss Bennet, I did not expect to see you again."

"Likewise," she said sweetly. Too sweetly, as her eyes said something else entirely. She was as unhappy about the situation as he was.

He wasn't certain why he'd come over now, for he could think of nothing to say, and what had seemed like a bit of pleasure at reminding her he was there now had the awkward effect of leaving them both uncomfortable. He was relieved when Richard stepped forward for introductions, and he quickly introduced his cousin to the other members of the party. His spine stiffened at the way Richard lifted Lizzy's hands, his lips deliberately hovering over her glove longer than necessary while he complimented her flushed cheeks and fine eyes.

Telling himself it wasn't jealousy, but rather alarm, he moved away from them to take a seat as the party started to seat itself in the sitting room. Lady Catherine dominated the space with her position in the thronelike chair, and he wondered if she had deliberately selected it because it sat higher than the others and seemed so luxuriant, or if it was simply her ostentatious taste.

He realized he was sitting beside his cousin, and he smiled at Anne. "How are you this evening?"

She hesitated for a long moment, as though she were trying to decide what to say. He was worried when he saw how pale she was, and there were bags under her eyes. "Are you well, Anne?" The poor dear had suffered bouts of illness since childhood.

After a moment, she blinked and managed a shaky smile. "I am quite well, Fitzwilliam. How are you?"

He shrugged a shoulder. "I am well." It was a rather stifled conversation, and though he had oftentimes spent hours engaged with Anne discussing various things, there was always a restrictive presence between them whenever they were around Lady Catherine. Her expectations of them becoming engaged weighed heavily on both of them, though Fitzwilliam was convinced Anne had as little interest in the union as he did.

It was still dreadfully annoying to have to be conscious of every interaction, certain Catherine was watching them and looking for signs only she would see that supported her belief they were getting closer, and he would inevitably ask for Anne's hand. That it had not occurred in the years since Anne was old enough did not seem to concern her too much just yet.

He was on tenterhooks, realizing he was waiting for Lizzy or someone to bring up the subject of what had happened in Meryton.

He could well imagine his aunt's reaction to learning he had been instrumental in helping to find a thief, and then later thwarting Georgiana's kidnapping.

She would likely be appalled by the investigation, but what would really bother her would be that Georgiana had been alone with her kidnapper, and Fitzwilliam hadn't forced a marriage. That was the sort of mindset his aunt had, so he wasn't eager for her to learn of the circumstances. He was determined to nip any such conversation in the bud, but he was pleasantly surprised when no one from Meryton broached the topic over dinner.

He managed to successfully avoid Lizzy for most of the meal, and for tea afterward. He and Richard didn't bother to excuse themselves for port, knowing they would have to take Mr. Collins along if they did. That was a prospect he didn't have the stomach for, so he followed the ladies back into the salon after dinner, pleased when Lizzy went to the pianoforte at his aunt's insistence.

"I seem to remember you play passably well, Miss Bennet?" she asked as she shooed her that way.

"Passably," said Lizzy with a twitch of her lips.

"You are welcome to use the pianoforte in Mrs. Jenkinson's parlor while you are visiting Hunsford. After all, one must practice to improve oneself."

Before she started to play, she sent Lady Catherine what appeared to be a genuine smile. "You must play quite well then, Lady Catherine?"

His aunt looked irritated for a moment before calm confidence filled her expression. "I never did have time to learn with all my other duties, but I do have quite an ear for music. I have no doubt I would have been a master if I had had the time to learn. Of course, Anne would have been as well, if she had not been such a sickly little thing." She made that sound like a moral failing on her daughter's part.

Fitzwilliam sent Anne a look of sympathy, but she appeared inured to her mother's comments. Before he could explain it to himself, he was drifting over to stand at the pianoforte, joining his cousin, who was there engaged in conversation with Lizzy as she arranged her sheet music before she started to play.

He wanted to speak with her. He was surprised by that, especially recalling how they had shouted at each other before the Netherfield ball. He'd hardly been in possession of his faculties the last time he saw her, only barely remembering most of their conversation. That she had hit him in the head while trying to help him had certainly scrambled his brains, but he wanted to talk with her again. Of course, he couldn't really do that while she was playing.

Her fingers started moving over the keys, and he was startled to realize she was better than he'd expected. She was nowhere near Georgiana's caliber, but he doubted she'd had the same access to masters his sister had enjoyed. When it came to enriching her talents and catering to her interests, he'd spared no expense for Georgiana. He imagined Lizzy could not have had even close to the same advantages. Considering what must've been her limited education, she played quite well, only missing a couple of the notes.

Despite Catherine's insistence she had quite a fine ear for music, she didn't seem to notice Lizzy's missteps, and when Lizzy had finished playing, she said, "That was quite lovely. I insist you must come over and practice on the pianoforte, for you obviously have raw talent, so it must be honed."

"That is a most generous offer," said Lizzy, not committing to the idea.

Fitzwilliam was amused to notice his aunt didn't seem to realize that. She nodded in satisfaction, clearly thinking the matter had been settled before turning to Mrs. Jenkinson. "You will, of course, make your pianoforte available to her." It was issued as a statement of fact.

Mrs. Jenkinson nodded her head. "Of course, Lady Catherine."

Lizzy seemed about to play them another piece, so while he had a chance, Darcy asked, "Are you well after the experience with Wickham?"

Her eyes widened slightly, and she dropped the page she was opening. While Richard fetched it for her, she said, "I am well. How are you, Mr. Darcy? Did you recover from your head injury?" She cringed as she asked, clearly still bearing some guilt.

He could've laughed, but he kept his reply non-accusatory when he said, "It was dreadfully painful for a few days, but it is better now."

"Not so painful that you could not travel by coach the morning after the ball and your injury," she said with a hint of reproof in her tone. Before he could respond, she said, "I do hope Miss Georgiana is well?"

He nodded. "She is. I saw her to Pemberley, where she wished to recover. She plans to join me in London in a short time, but for now, she needs her rest." He pitched his voice low as Richard handed her the sheet music, realizing she was about to start playing again. "I would appreciate your discretion about that, Miss Bennet. My aunt has no knowledge of Georgiana's incident, and I would like to keep it that way."

Lizzy looked up at him with a frown. "I shan't say a word. Surely, she cannot hold that against her?"

He shrugged a shoulder. "She has a peculiar way of thinking at times. For example, she is most insistent I will eventually marry Anne."

"She must be dreadfully disappointed if you have not told her yet." Her expression closed, and her tone turned cool.

He couldn't fathom why, but before he had a chance to respond, she began to play enthusiastically. She practically threw herself into it, though it seemed to cause her to make more mistakes than she had before. When she had finished that song, she stood up, saying, "I believe my fingers are too stiff to continue playing. My apologies, Lady Catherine."

"I do understand. Of course, once you have practiced more on the pianoforte, you shall be able to play us an entire concert, I have no doubt. That should occur before you leave, Miss Bennet."

If Lizzy found her vote of confidence sustaining, she didn't show it. She merely appeared amused when she said, "Of course, Lady Catherine."

Darcy couldn't help following her as she returned to the sitting room, taking a seat near her in the armchair after she sat by Anne. She didn't speak to him for a moment, and then her shoulders straightened, and he braced himself, knowing something unpleasant was coming when she turned to face him. In a polite tone, she asked, "How is Mr. Bingley?"

"He is well. He has returned to London and sees no reason to go back to Netherfield. It is unlikely he will extend his tenancy there." He spoke the words formally, interjecting confidence in them he wasn't entirely certain he felt.

While Charles was back in London, his friend was moping, and Darcy was afraid he might yet give in to his feelings and try to approach Jane. He was doing his best to keep his friend from returning to Netherfield, so he was relieved the weather would turn and make it difficult to travel soon.

"How fortuitous. My sister Jane is in London as well."

"You have a sister?" asked Richard as he came to join them, sitting on Anne's other side.

"I have four sisters, but the one of interest is Jane."

Fitzwilliam stiffened at the words. "What brings Miss Jane to London?"

"She is visiting our aunt and uncle. She will likely stay past Christmas, and I am on my way to join her after I visit with Charlotte for a while."

His blood ran cold at the thought, and he resolved he would warn Charles to be on his guard. He might also send a note to Caroline

Bingley to warn her as well. Though he didn't want her to get any ideas, he couldn't deny her assistance, along with Louisa's, had been instrumental in helping them convince Charles there was nothing for him at Netherfield, and that his perception of Miss Jane was wrong. It couldn't hurt to warn her to be aware. In fact, it was more sensible to warn her and circumvent Bingley. With luck, his friend would never learn Jane was there.

AFTER THE COLLINS COUPLE and their guests had departed, Fitzwilliam lingered long enough to avail himself of the writing desk in a sitting room, sitting down to pen a note to Caroline Bingley, giving her a warning about Jane's presence. He was sealing the wax when Richard came to join him.

"What are you up to, Darcy?"

"I am sending a message. There is an unsuitable woman who is trying to catch Mr. Bingley's eye, and I feel it is incumbent upon me to issue a warning."

Richard sighed. "As vexing as it is to have to find an heiress, there are times when I do not envy you or Mr. Bingley your positions. It must be trying to never know if a woman wants you for your money or yourself."

"Indeed." Darcy couldn't help thinking of Lizzy at that moment, though it was wildly inappropriate. He supposed there was something refreshing about her. She didn't want him under any circumstances, either for money or love. While he was relieved by the former, he was disconcerted to find himself not happily embracing the latter.

Of course, it would be an ego boost if she bore tender feelings for him, but there was nothing more to it than that, he assured himself. The same impediments existed that always had. Her family would be a burden, and she was not the sort of wife he would ever seek.

Chapter Three

Lizzy was walking through Rosings Park the next morning, admiring the beauty of the grounds. Lady Catherine's landscapers must be skilled, and she had no doubt they were numerous to keep the large estate looking so pristine.

She couldn't help contrasting the size of Rosings Park with Longbourn Park, though the comparison was laughable. The entirety of Longbourn would likely fit in the field she was standing in now. It was a lovely place, though it would've been lovelier if it didn't have Lady Catherine attached to it.

She looked up at a shrill sound, realizing there was someone approaching and whistling as he walked. She was certain it wasn't Darcy, but she disapproved of the way her heart leapt at the idea even as she turned to identify the person approaching.

It was Richard Fitzwilliam, and the colonel paused as he neared, bending at the waist. "I did not expect to see anyone while out for my morning constitutional, Miss Bennet."

She smiled. "I tend to be an early riser, and my day is better if I greet it with a walk."

He nodded. "Very sensible of you. I share a similar approach." He extended his arm. "Shall we walk together?"

She smiled. "Why not?" Threading her arm through his, she fell into step with the colonel, who proved to be an amusing man with a lighthearted sense of humor, and a sparkling wit. He was completely charming, and she wished she felt more inclined to be charmed. Perhaps it was simply after her experience with Wickham that she distrusted charming superficiality, though Colonel Fitzwilliam didn't appear to be overly shallow.

"Are you betrothed, Miss Bennet?" asked the colonel as they walked.

Lizzy laughed. "No, fortunately I have avoided that fate thus far."

His eyebrows drew together in feigned astonishment. "Could it be there is such a creature in the world?"

She frowned. "What do you mean?"

He grinned. "A woman who is not interested in matrimony? I find it scarcely believable."

Lizzy laughed. "I am that rare creature indeed. I would never marry for anything but love."

The man beside her sighed. "Would that I had that luxury."

She frowned. "Why would you not, Colonel? Your father is an Earl."

"He is, but the difference is I am the second son of the earl. I will not be inheriting vast lands and a full coffer. Of course, my father will leave me an annuity, but it is generally expected I shall make my own way in the world. I do not mind being a soldier overly much, but I do not wish to maintain this as my career forever. That necessitates finding an heiress to marry if I wish to remain in a comfortable station in life. I will be unlikely to find an heiress that I love, so I must compromise my morals and marry for money instead of true affection." He spoke as though it were a dire fate, but he was practically laughing.

Lizzy laughed along with him. "You poor dear. You must suffer ever so much to ensure you have the finer things in life."

"I see you understand me. I do not suppose you are an heiress, Miss Bennet?" he asked with an exaggerated leer.

She giggled in spite of herself. "Hardly, much to your disappointment, I am certain, Colonel. I am positive my inadequate dowry is scarcely the amount required to keep you in luxury."

"Pity," he said, looking crestfallen, though it had to be exaggerated. After a moment, he sighed, looking unexpectedly serious. "I jest about my need for an heiress, but perhaps it is better to be the one seeking wealth than the one whose wealth is sought."

She frowned. "What do you mean?"

"Take my cousin Darcy, and his friend Bingley. Both men of fine incomes, so they are naturally targets of women who want to elevate their station in life. Just last evening, Darcy had to pen a warning to his friend about a predatory female in London. I would rather be the hunter than the hunted."

Lizzy gritted her teeth and managed a polite smile. "I am certain that would be the better position." She said the words without enthusiasm, though she tried to sound neutral when she asked, "The friend was Mr. Bingley, I take it, since you mentioned him?"

He nodded. "I do not know the circumstances, but it must be dreadful to fear avid pursuit and never know if a woman wants you or your money."

"I suspect if you are the one with the money, you would take that concern in stride, Colonel Fitzwilliam. It must be a small problem with which to deal when one has an excessive income." She marveled at how carefree she sounded, but she was seething with anger inside.

After her walk with the colonel ended, Lizzy knew she should return to Hunsford, but her feet took her in the direction of Rosings Park instead. It was too early to be calling on anyone, but she was too angry to pay much attention to decorum at the moment. Once again, Darcy revealed his meddling. How could he continue to try to thwart Jane's happiness because he was arrogant enough to believe he understood other people's hearts?

Enraged, she knocked on the front door and didn't wait for the butler to allow her in. She just walked past him and said, "I am here to see Fitzwilliam Darcy. Retrieve him please."

The butler stiffened his posture and looked like he might argue, but when Lizzy glared at him, his courage failed, and he nodded. "Please wait in the first sitting room, Miss Bennet."

That indicated he knew who she was, so perhaps that explained why he had given her a little leeway. She figured it was more likely because she was in a mood that suggested he not trifle with her, and she couldn't hide that—though she'd made little effort to disguise it, truthfully.

She turned to the sitting room, pacing as she waited for Darcy to join her. He was surprisingly quick about it, and she was startled to see he hadn't bothered with a jacket. His sleeves were rolled to the elbows as well, and she was unexpectedly flustered at the sight of his forearms for an instant before she recalled why she was there.

She waited until the butler closed the door after they declined tea before marching toward him. "Did you send Mr. Bingley a letter warning him to avoid Jane?"

He frowned. "How did you hear of that?"

"Your cousin revealed it this morning. I doubt he understood it was my sister you are warning Mr. Bingley against, for he seemed to think it was a burden you poor wealthy men must endure, to never know if a woman loved your money or you."

He flinched for a moment, but then his shoulders stiffened. "I did send a missive to warn Miss Caroline. I know she will watch out for Charles's interest."

"No doubt, for she wishes to please you." Lizzy was enraged, wishing she knew exactly what to say to make Darcy withdraw his interference. She had tried appealing to him before, asking him to reevaluate his opinion, but that was a lost cause. She realized she was here to vent her spleen, though nothing she said was likely to influence him. "I do loathe you, Mr. Darcy. You are so sanctimonious and certain of everyone and everything. You believe you can move people around like pieces on a chessboard to suit your stratagems. Your hubris is astounding."

His expression tightened, and he glared down at her. "You are impertinent. I do not require your approval or your opinion, Miss Bennet. I have made clear my feelings on the matter. I will do my utmost to protect my friend from the grasp of your sister."

"And I shall do everything in my power to stop your interference." She glared up at him, chest heaving in her anger. "How dare you be so callous? You would break my sister's heart without a thought."

"I do not believe that for a moment. She would break my friend's heart once he accepts she does not love him if he offers for her. I will not see him trapped in a marriage lacking love and passion."

"You do not see anything you do not wish to see, Darcy." She almost shouted the words at him, struggling to maintain control and keep her voice modulated. "You are determined to see her as a fortune seeker, so that is all you observe. You are so stubborn and intractable you can never contemplate the idea you might be wrong. I almost wish the branch I used had done you in."

"Perhaps you are ready to concede it was not an accident? No doubt, you were helping Wickham escape."

Lizzy's mouth dropped open at the accusation, and though she realized he was probably using her own fears against her to get a rise out of her, she was incapable of speaking. Instead, she lifted her hand with every intention of slapping him, but his hand intercepted her wrist before she could.

She lifted her other hand to try again, and he held that wrist as well. "I have no affection for Wickham, and I did nothing to help him deliberately. I am just sorry I did not remove you, for it would allow my sister to be happy." She struggled to escape his hands as she spoke.

"You are such a ferocious creature and nothing at all like a lady should be. Curse you, Elizabeth Bennet." As he said the words, Darcy bent his head, and Lizzy gasped with rage when his mouth pressed against hers. She started to fight him, but a strange indolence took over her limbs, as though dragging them to the ground.

She slumped against him, and his arms wrapped around her after releasing her wrists. She clasped the lapels of his waistcoat, shocking herself by opening her mouth as his tongue darted inside. It was an explosive kiss, and she'd never been kissed at all, let alone like this.

After a moment, she couldn't determine which one of them regained their senses, but they seemed to pull apart at roughly the same time.

"You cannot influence me in any fashion to believe Jane is sincere in her affections for Bingley. Do not try such a thing again, Miss Bennet." He spoke coldly.

She was once more on the verge of slapping him. "You are the one who kissed me, Mr. Darcy. You need not imagine I was trying to manipulate you in some fashion. If you ever touch me again, I shall scream down the house."

With those words, she turned on her heel and started to leave, pausing only long enough to say, "You might believe you know how others think and feel, but you are fooling yourself, Mr. Darcy. You are not the judge of character you imagine. You should be ashamed of yourself for trying to sew unhappiness and discontent everywhere you go. I should not be surprised though, for it seems to come naturally to you."

With those words, she passed through the doorway, intent on a dignified departure. Her lips still burned where he'd touched them, and his taste lingered in her mouth. It was the most peculiar thing, and it should have been unpleasant, but she couldn't force herself to regard the kiss in that light.

The aftermath and the emotions preceding it had been anything but pleasant, but the kiss itself had been astounding. She had not realized she could ever feel like that, and she wondered what other delights awaited. Perhaps she was too hasty in her decision not to marry unless it was for deep love. Of course, she could never love a man like Fitzwilliam Darcy, but perhaps there were compensations to marriage—to anyone but him—she had failed to contemplate until now.

Chapter Four

Lizzy was leaving when she heard crying, and it arrested her intent to march out of Rosings Park with her head held high and her shoulders straight. She couldn't ignore the sound of suffering, so she followed it and found herself in the chapel seconds later. There was a slight figure kneeling at the altar, and it was from her the tears were coming. Lizzy rushed forward, recognizing Anne when she knelt beside her. "Whatever is troubling you, Miss Anne?"

Anne turned to her, tears staining her cheeks. Her face was unusually flushed, and though it was becoming on her, that her misery had prompted the change in appearance made it undesirable. Lizzy grasped her shoulders, hugging her gently. "You may tell me whatever bothers you. I shall not reveal your secrets to anyone."

"Oh, Miss Eliza, it is dreadful."

Those were the only words Lizzy managed to get out of Anne for the next few minutes as the young woman continued to cry on her shoulder, tears gradually slowing as Lizzy rocked her back and forth while gently rubbing her back. "What troubles you, Anne?"

"This," Anne finally said with a sniffle and a hiccup as she handed over a letter.

Lizzy opened it, finding it difficult to read a few parts because the ink was smeared from tears. From what she could piece together, someone was demanding a payment to keep Anne's secret. She looked up at the young woman, frowning. "What secret?" It seemed to defy belief that Anne de Bourgh could be doing something that would open her to extortion.

Anne bit her lip. "I cannot say. I am not certain how I will pay this person. I managed the payment last time, and I have just enough this time, but after that, I do not know how I will manage to make another payment, and I am sure the demand will come again. The last letter assured me it was the only time the blackmailer would request payment for silence, yet here he has sent another one again this month."

Lizzy read the letter once more, realizing it alluded to a designated drop point, directing her to leave it in the same place as last time. "You plan to pay the man then?"

She frowned. "Is it a man?"

Lizzy hesitated. "To be honest, I have no indication either way." She looked down at the writing, which was thick and blocky, and certainly not feminine, but that didn't mean the writer was a man. Her own mother had dreadful handwriting, while her father had pristine loops that could've been penned by the finest ladies in the land. She couldn't tell for certain based on the shaping of the letters what the gender was of the person who'd written the letter. "Do you have an idea who might be blackmailing you?"

"Yes," said Anne. She didn't sound confident though. "Someone who knows my secret."

That was hardly a promising start. Lizzy bit back a sigh of impatience. "What is your secret?"

"It is shameful. You shall think I am a terrible person."

Lizzy frowned. "I cannot imagine that, Anne." She'd fallen into using her first name with easy familiarity, hoping to soothe the girl and reinforce the bond of trust growing between them. "Likely, whatever you have done is little more than a youthful indiscretion. With your mother's level of wealth and standing, silence is virtually guaranteed."

Anne shook her head. "She cannot find out. If she does, she will destroy him."

Lizzy froze. "Who?"

"Carlos," said Anne softly. "He is the Spanish groom my mother hired last year because of his excellent references. She managed to entice him away from a *duque* in Spain, but she won't hesitate to destroy him if she realizes..." She trailed off, closing her eyes as tears streamed down her cheeks again.

"You and Carlos are...friends?" asked Lizzy delicately.

"So much more than friends, Eliza." She seemed pained as she made the admission. "I would marry him tomorrow if I could, but I know what my mother would do to him. She would destroy Carlos, and she might banish me. I tried to convince Carlos to run away with me last month when I got the first demand for money, but he is too honorable. He refuses to consign me to a life of hiding."

Lizzy wasn't certain he was being entirely noble. Perhaps he simply didn't want to live that kind of life either, but she didn't point that out to Anne. "Do you have the request from last month?"

Anne nodded as she reached into her pocket, pulling out another letter. "I have been carrying it with me, for I cannot risk having someone find it, but I could not bear to throw it away either. I entertained the idea of perhaps hiring a Runner to find out who is trying to blackmail me, but I could not figure out how to do that."

Lizzy folded the letters together. "May I keep these for a short time?"

Anne frowned. "Why?"

Lizzy straightened her shoulders. "I am not a Runner, but I do have some talent for putting together the pieces of a mystery. If you will entrust me with these letters, I will endeavor to find out who is blackmailing you so we can put a stop to it."

She looked uncertain for a moment, but when Lizzy squeezed her hand in a reassuring fashion, she nodded as she hiccupped again. "I... I suppose. You will not tell anyone, will you?"

Lizzy shook her head vehemently. "Never. You have my utmost discretion, I assure you. I will not breathe a word of your relationship to anyone, and I most certainly will not mention your blackmailer. I will do my best to find him, and if I cannot, I will try to help you engage a Runner."

Anne looked hopeful for the first time since Lizzy had found her crying in the chapel. "Bless you, Eliza. I hope you can do what you say."

Lizzy hugged her, wishing fervently for the same. She didn't want to make a false promise to Anne. It was her sincere hope she could identify the blackmailer and get the situation in hand when she had his or her identity, but even if it proved beyond her, she was determined to help. She might not be able to find the blackmailer, but she could certainly get a Runner for Anne when she traveled on to London in a few weeks.

She hoped to put the matter to rest before then, and Lizzy was startled to realize she was looking forward to the challenge. She was appalled at whatever was lacking in this person's moral makeup to allow them to create such a horrid scheme to deploy against Anne, who had little happiness as it was. She was determined to expose them without exposing Anne, but she relished the challenge of doing so, both for justice and for her own curiosity.

Lizzy excused herself from Anne a short time later, deciding she needed to speak with Carlos as well. She hoped he would be receptive to conversation, and she made her way to the stables. Not being much of a horsewoman, her anxiety increased as she neared the stables, and the horrible thought occurred to her that perhaps Carlos was the one blackmailing his lover.

Maybe he wanted to get a payoff so he could afford to leave, and he'd seduced sweet Anne with that plan in mind. She was predisposed to dislike him as she entered the stables, quickly identifying who she thought might be Carlos by his swarthy complexion and dark black hair, along with a neat beard and mustache. She approached him, trying to sound polite, though she had halfway convicted him in her mind already. "Are you Carlos?"

He nodded as he bowed to her. "I am. How may I help you, miss?"

"I know about you and Anne," she said quietly.

His demeanor changed, moving from obsequious to angry in seconds. He was practically in her face a moment later. "You are the blackmailer. What an underhanded, dastardly person you must be. I demand you leave Anne alone. If you were a man, I would call you out."

His aggression made her take a step back, but there had been an accusatory note in her own tone, so she could hardly fault him for reacting so strongly when he'd assumed she was the blackmailer. She was actually pleased he had done so, because it indicated he was protective of Anne, and she was able to mostly dismiss her semi-formed theory that he might be blackmailing his lover.

She lifted a hand, making her voice more soothing. "I am not the blackmailer, and I am not here to threaten you, Carlos. I simply wanted to know if you had any information that might help me identify who is blackmailing her."

His anger faded slightly, and he took a step back. He seemed to be trapped between disbelief and relief for a moment as he stared at her. "You are not here to expose us?"

Lizzy shook her head. "I am not. It is my belief Anne needs every bit of happiness she can find, and if you make her happy, it matters naught to me what your station or position is. I figure she has enough money for both of you."

His shoulders stiffened again. "I am not with her because of money, miss." His words were cold, his rage underscoring them. "I know what someone like you would believe, but—"

Lizzy lifted her hand again. "You do not need to defend yourself to me. I certainly did not intend to insult you in any fashion, Carlos." It was strange to use his first name, but she'd never learned his last name from Anne, and she didn't want to interrupt the flow of conversation to exchange greetings and introductions. "I simply want to help. If you love her, I am pleased, for I worried there was more to your actions than simply caring about her."

He still looked stiff, but he sounded surprisingly unoffended when he said, "You assumed I was blackmailing her after seducing her?"

Lizzy bit her lip as she nodded, wondering if she should be so blunt with her admission of the truth, since it was just the two of them in the stables. Despite his initial aggressive reaction, she realized she didn't feel afraid of him. "The thought occurred to me."

His shoulders slumped slightly. "That is why I tell her we cannot truly be together. There will always be someone who assumes we are together for my nefarious reasons, or because she is a fool. I do love Anne, but she deserves someone better than me."

Lizzy scowled at him. "Love seems like the most fundamental component one needs, Carlos. Do not let the judgment of others keep you from happiness."

He seemed to be mulling over her words as he nodded, but he didn't address them directly. Instead, he said, "I can only infer someone must have observed us at an inopportune time. Miss Anne has her regular morning rides, and we are sometimes able to have a few minutes alone together. Otherwise, there are nights when she sneaks out to see me in my quarters outside the stables."

He flushed at the words. "You must not think ill of her. I would marry her if I could, but that is more dishonorable than what we are currently doing, for marrying her would bring her nothing but misery."

Lizzy frowned at him. "I think it would bring her happiness, Carlos."

He sighed heavily. "Until her mother disowns her, or until Lady Catherine orders me to be murdered, and I disappear. I can see no way for us to be together, but the compulsion draws us together anyway. I cannot bring myself to send her away, though I love her and know it would be better for her."

She realized there was little she could do to persuade him, but she hoped Anne would have better luck convincing him not to be so noble. Instead, she said, "So you think it is someone who might have observed you during your rides, or perhaps seen her slip out at night?" At his nod, she allowed her thoughts to focus on that, though it did little to bring her a clue of the identity of the blackmailer. It could've been any number of people on the estate, or even people adjacent to the estate.

With a sigh, she said, "I have told Anne I will try my best to find the blackmailer, and I intend to do so."

He looked hopeful. "I hope you can do so, for it rests heavily on her."

"So does the indecision of the relationship, I would imagine. It must be difficult for both of you to be constantly fighting what you feel. Perhaps you would both do better to accept it and fight *for* it."

Carlos looked grim. "It is easy to say that from an outsider's perspective, but if I were to be intractable, to dig in and insist on making Anne my bride as is our wish, how would her mother react? What might she do, and not just to me? You must think me cowardly, but I am not. I am trying to be pragmatic. If Lady de Bourgh killed me, it would destroy Anne, but you do not know the depths of the woman's rage. I fear she might destroy Anne as well in her need for vengeance. That is why I cannot give in to Anne's pleas to run away, or to marry her. Perhaps things will be different when Lady Catherine dies."

"I certainly hope so." Lizzy licked her lips, wondering if she dared ask an indelicate question. "What if there were to be a child from your liaison, Carlos?"

He flushed, clearly not wishing to discuss the subject. "There are ways to prevent that. That is all you need to know, miss."

Lizzy was content with that explanation, and she took her leave from Carlos a short time later. She hadn't learned anything particularly useful for identifying the blackmailer, but at least she was able to confidently strike Carlos from the list.

She wished he would be bolder and accept Anne's offer to run away, but she could see the pragmatic reasons not to as well. He seemed to genuinely fear Lady de Bourgh as well, and she couldn't blame him. The woman was fierce, and Lizzy wouldn't want to be standing between what Lady de Bourgh desired and her getting it.

SHE WALKED FOR A BIT, trying to think, but she wasn't certain how to put together the pieces. What seemed the most logical course was to show up at the drop point and watch for the blackmailer to pick up the package, and that was her plan as she made her way back to the rectory.

She was surprised to find a wagon parked in front of the rectory, and there were four burly men carrying stacks of marble to the back garden. She paused by it, admiring how pretty the marble was as Mr. Collins oversaw the dispersal. "No, put that pile over there. Yes, right there. It will be much easier for me to position the tiles. Thank you, my good men."

He was too preoccupied with his order to pay much attention to Lizzy, so she slipped past him and entered the rectory. She found Charlotte in the sitting room, and her friend asked, "Have you had breakfast?"

Lizzy started to answer, but her stomach rumbling replied for her. "I believe I completely forgot it. I got engrossed in my walk."

Charlotte frowned in disapproval. "I thought you were out rather longer than usual. The grounds around the area are lovely though. I shall ring for Mrs. Tesch to bring you a tray."

"Thank you. That is most thoughtful." Lizzy sat down and poured herself a cup of tea from the tray in front of Charlotte as she waited for breakfast. "Speaking of lovely, it looks like Mr. Collins will be renovating his garden again." It was a usual project she had seen him undertake many times during her visits.

Charlotte rolled her eyes, but with a hint of gentle enjoyment. "It keeps him busy for many hours each day, so of course, I heartily endorse it."

"The marble is very fine indeed. I am surprised Mr. Collins could acquire such a thing."

Charlotte waved a hand. "I have no doubt it was either a castoff from Lady Catherine, or she decided Hunsford's garden was too shabby and must match the splendor of Rosings Park. There is no declining a gift from Lady de Bourgh when she is insistent upon giving it, regardless of the wish of one to receive it or not," said Charlotte with a little twitch of her lips.

Lizzy laughed. "I can well see that about Lady Catherine, and of course, Mr. Collins would never reject any offering from his patroness."

Charlotte shook her head as Mrs. Tesch brought in a tray. "Undeniably, he would not, for Lady Catherine is correct in all things." The two women dissolved into giggles for a moment, and Lizzy saw Mrs. Tesch grinning like she wanted to join in as she left the room. Likely, the housekeeper had at least heard enough about Lady de Bourgh, if she had not met her, to appreciate their humor and understand its origin.

Chapter Five

Darcy spent that day and most of the next pacing and fretting, unable not to think about the kiss he had exchanged with Miss Bennet. He had been the one to instigate it, but she certainly hadn't pushed him away. He'd never expected to discover such passion with her, and that he couldn't stop thinking about the exchange was vexing.

No matter how he tried to remind himself how unsuitable she was, going so far as to continuously list her shortcomings and her family's faults in his mind as he carried on his business throughout that day and the next, he couldn't seem to convince himself kissing her had been little more than tolerable.

It had been life-altering, and he was forced to evaluate his interactions with her in a new light. It was disconcerting to realize there was more than attraction involved in the situation. He had come to care for Lizzy. Perhaps more than care for her. When he first had that realization hours after the kiss, he immediately rejected it as nonsense. He was far too wise to do such a foolish thing as to fall in love with a woman like Elizabeth Bennet.

For all her failings, she was quite a woman though. With her intelligence and quiet beauty, along with her ability to engage his senses in every way, it was hardly surprising he had formed a *tendre* for her.

When he realized that, he accepted it with a little less hostility that time, though he still tried to forget it. He continued to reject the concept, but as the thought kept returning to him throughout the day and into the next, he reluctantly reached the conclusion he loved Lizzy Bennet.

He couldn't pinpoint exactly when it'd happened, but there was no denying he felt it. He loved her to the extent she preoccupied his thoughts, and she was leading him to all manner of actions he'd never considered before. For goodness sake, he'd investigated the thefts with her, and he had spent time with her alone for hours in the woods as they waited for Wickham to arrive at the shed, hoping to identify him.

He'd kissed her in his aunt's sitting room after exchanging angry words with her, and that hadn't even been the first time they had argued so vehemently. If he couldn't break free of his misplaced adoration, he would likely not recognize himself within a year.

That was enough to help him resist for a while longer, but within two days of having kissed her, he found himself resigned to the state of loving her, and furthermore, he didn't think he could be happy without her. It was a galling position in which to find himself, but he was determined to face up to the truth, so he set out that morning with the intent of finding her, hoping she still maintained her morning walks even while visiting Hunsford.

He felt like he had been over half of the property before he finally caught sight of her sitting against a tree on a hill. He approached quietly, not with the intent to sneak up on her, but simply because he was still trying to talk himself out of this course of action. As a consequence, she didn't realize he was there until he had a chance to read the letter over her shoulder.

His mouth dropped open in shock as he read the allegations against her. She was engaging in an affair with a groom at Rosings Park. He could hardly imagine her brazenness, let alone the speed at which she moved. She'd only been a guest in the area for a week or so.

He was appalled, not just that she could behave so recklessly, but that someone had already picked up on her actions. She had ruined everything, and he couldn't hold back his anger when he marched around to face her. "What kind of low character do you have, Miss Bennet?"

Her eyes widened at the accusation as she jumped to her feet, hastily folding the letter. He realized there was a second one as well. She glared at him with her hands on her hips. "Whatever are you on about now, Mr. Darcy?"

He gestured to the letter. "You are having an affair, and someone is demanding payment to keep quiet." Her eyes narrowed as she looked down at the letter, and then she laughed at him. It almost brought his fury to a boiling point, and he had to take several deep breaths to maintain control.

"I am not the one being blackmailed, Mr. Darcy, but I should hardly be surprised you would think I am."

He arched a brow in skepticism. "You are the one holding the letter, and the contents are damning."

"I offered my assistance to the injured party to find the blackmailer. I assure you, it is not me." She spoke with proud confidence, her shoulders stiff as she glared up at him. "It is not your concern either way."

He crossed his arms over his chest. "Tell me who is being blackmailed then?" He was hardly surprised when she shook her head. "Because there is no one besides you. You are the guilty party."

Her eyes widened, and she looked incensed. "If I were the one being blackmailed, I would be the victim, not the guilty party."

He snorted. "A woman who cavorts with a groom, one she could hardly know, is very much to blame for her situation if she is blackmailed because of it."

She glared at him, practically seething with enmity. "You are once more passing judgment and making condemnations. Yet again, you do not fully grasp the situation, but you are quick to rush in with conclusions. It must be quite painful to be so narrowminded and rigid, Mr. Darcy." With those words, she turned and marched away from him.

He wanted to rush after her, to continue the confrontation, but he was certain she wouldn't say anything to him now. No, he would simply turn up where she was supposed to meet her blackmailer and discover the full sordidness of the situation for himself. He would rescue her if he could, but her deeds proved once again he couldn't maintain the course of action he had decided upon earlier in the morning when he'd set out to find her. He had been a fool, but this incident brought him back to his senses, at least enough to realize it.

HE WAS DISMAYED TO see the Collins couple and their guests were at Rosings Park for dinner again that night, and he did his best to avoid interacting with Lizzy in any fashion. She seemed equally determined to ignore him, and she took a seat at the table far away from him. As dinner progressed, he kept finding his gaze wandering to her, though he tried to forbid it to do so.

At first, he was so angry with her that it took him a little while to realize she was deep in quiet conversation with Anne, who looked distraught. Suddenly, it occurred to him maybe he had misjudged Lizzy, and perhaps she was genuinely helping someone else. Could that be his cousin?

He could hardly credit the idea due to her ill-health, and the iron fist with which Lady Catherine ruled her, but it also seemed preposterous in retrospect to think Lizzy might be engaging in an illicit affair with a groom she'd known less than a week. He was confused, but he was determined to keep an eye on the situation, and he observed after dinner that the women continued to speak quietly over tea, at least until Lady Catherine admonished them about whispering together and being rude. After that, their conversation was more generally engaged with everyone, and the guests left a while later.

He waited until Lady Catherine was busy getting herself together before approaching Anne, saying softly, "Are you all right?"

She looked at him with her eyes wide, and her expression haunted. "I am fine," she said in a tone that wasn't at all convincing. "Why do you ask?"

"I did not realize you were such good friends with Elizabeth Bennet?" He phrased it as a question.

She shrugged. "She is a lovely young woman, and I enjoy conversing with her." Anne opened her fan and started furiously waving it in front of her pale face. "If you will excuse me, Fitzwilliam, I find myself dreadfully tired this evening. I believe I will retire now."

He nodded his head. "I hope you sleep well, Cousin."

When Anne had left the drawing room, Fitzwilliam went with Richard, and they returned to their own quarters. He waited a little while before slipping out again, not bothering to have his valet help him undress. He suspected he might still need his clothing yet.

He sat in the darkened drawing room, which provided a good view of the hallway leading to the front door. He heard footsteps on the stairs a short time later and wasn't surprised to see a small, slight figure slip into view. Despite the cloak obscuring her, he was positive it was Anne.

She slipped out the front door, and he waited a couple of moments before following her. Once outside, he saw her easily enough even with the cloak, and he followed at a discreet distance to verify where she went. He waited until she had crossed the grounds and disappeared behind the stables before returning to the house. Her actions confirmed his supposition. Anne, not Lizzy, was the blackmail victim.

He groaned softly as he recalled his words to Lizzy, issued from jealousy and anger. They were far more condemnatory than he felt about his cousin's actions. In light of the life Anne had lived, he could hardly fault her for finding some happiness, even if the man was wildly inappropriate.

He'd not been prepared to extend the same understanding to Lizzy, and he squirmed as he made his way back to his quarters, realizing how unfair he had been. He owed Lizzy an apology, and he intended to issue it forthwith. He also intended to offer his assistance, though he imagined she might protest.

In good conscience, he couldn't allow her to face the possibility of running into a blackmailer alone, but he knew Lizzy well enough to know she wouldn't be dissuaded from the course she had set, and the promise she'd given to his cousin to try to find out who was extorting her.

Her loyalty was one of the things he admired about her, and now that he realized how he had misjudged her, he was once again able to focus on her good traits and return his resolve to stay the course he had set earlier in the day. Perhaps he was still a fool, but that wasn't enough to dissuade him now that he knew the truth.

Chapter Six

Lizzy could barely hide her dismay when Fitzwilliam Darcy stepped into the sitting room at Hunsford the next day, though she hoped she managed a polite smile. Their last exchange still weighed heavily on her, making her voice cooler than normal when she said, "Good afternoon, Mr. Darcy."

He bent his head to her in a respectful fashion. "Good afternoon, Miss Bennet." He turned his attention to Charlotte. "Good afternoon, Mrs. Collins."

If Charlotte were startled by her visitor—and she must be, for what possible reason would Darcy have to call at Hunsford during teatime—she barely showed it in her manner. Instead, she got to her feet and went over to stand near him, giving him a bright smile. "How marvelous to see you, Mr. Darcy. We were about to enjoy tea. Will you sit with us?"

"I would be honored," said Darcy as he sat down.

Charlotte smiled at both of them. "If you shall excuse me for a moment, I will ask Mrs. Tesch to fetch another cup and saucer for us."

Sensing he wanted to speak with her alone, and Charlotte had likely realized that since she was going to speak with Mrs. Tesch instead of ringing the bell, Lizzy said, "You might want to check on Maria as well. The poor dear had such a terrible tummy ache from the fish."

Charlotte frowned, her concern for her younger sister obvious. "Yes, you are quite right. I shall return shortly." There was a hint of knowing in Charlotte's gaze that suggested she understood Lizzy was requesting time alone with Mr. Darcy. She probably had no idea why, but no doubt, she was imagining something fanciful, like romantic reasons.

Lizzy almost laughed aloud at the thought, but she maintained silence and composure until her friend had left the sitting room. Then she turned to glare at Darcy. "Why are you here?"

"I could pretend I came by for tea, but we both know the topic I wish to discuss."

"Perhaps you would like to chastise me further about my illicit relationships and ability to be blackmailed upon such short arrival? Or perhaps I have indulged in this affair with the groom for the many years I have been coming to visit Charlotte? That is six visits in total, counting this one. I might have seduced all manner of gentlemen around this part of the country."

Rather than look uncomfortable or even chastised, Darcy irritated her by laughing. "I do not underestimate your charm and skill, Miss Bennet, but I have realized the error of my ways. I know who the victim of the blackmail attempt is, and I come to offer my assistance."

Her eyes widened, but she refused to fall for the trap. "Certainly, you know," she said in a sarcastic voice. "You have only one wish, and that is for me to reveal the name to confirm your supposition, correct?"

His eyes widened, as though he was surprised she didn't believe him. Did he know her at all? Did he recall any of their interactions? She shook her head at his obliviousness.

"It is my dear cousin Anne, is it not? She is the one involved with the groom." He said the words calmly, as though Anne lowering herself to be with a servant didn't besmirch the family name and reflect badly on him.

Her mouth dropped open in shock. "How did you discover that?"

"I saw the two of you whispering quite conspiratorially last night, so I waited up to see if Anne sneaked out. She did and went to the stables. After that, I returned to the house, for I had no wish to further intrude upon her privacy."

Lizzy could barely understand the words coming from his mouth. "You confirmed it and did nothing to stop it?"

He shrugged a shoulder. "Why should I? I figure my cousin deserves some happiness, and though I am surprised she has found it with a groom, it is hardly likely to be revealed. If it were, that would be a catastrophe, for Lady Catherine would not take it well. Other than Lady Catherine learning of the affair, there is only one possibility that truly concerns me."

Inferring his meaning, she said, "I understand there are ways to prevent getting with child." She blurted it out before realizing how inappropriate her statement was. Her face flushed, and she opened her fan to wave it at her face in a frenzy. "I cannot believe I said that." What was wrong with her?

Darcy looked shock for a moment, but then his lips twitched with amusement. "I am surprised a woman of your standing knows that, but yes, there are methods. I assume Anne revealed that to you?"

Lizzy's face flushed even hotter. "It was Carlos," she said in a low voice, reluctantly admitting the truth.

He frowned. "It was Carlos?"

"He is her lover." The word hung between them, and it heightened her discomfort. "I challenged him about his willingness to hide his relationship with your cousin, asking what if there were a child, and he assured me that would not happen. It was a very awkward conversation, at least as awkward as this one."

If he was bothered by the discomfort of their current discussion, he didn't seem inclined to reveal that. Rather, he frowned sternly at her. "You should not have interrogated the groom alone. He could be the one behind the blackmail attempt."

Lizzy was impressed with his thought processes, which she hated to admit. "I did think of that, but I firmly believe we can rule him out." How naturally she had fallen into saying *we* about the investigation. There was certainly a comfortable familiarity about working with

Darcy, despite the animosity between them. She could rely on him to have a sound mind and steady nerves, which were both essential skills for investigating such matters, even if he did have a ridiculously delicate spot that made him vulnerable to attack.

"How can you be sure?" asked Darcy.

"He was quite convincing. He betrayed no sign of lying and acknowledged the theory as a possibility. I am certain he is not the one extorting Anne." She almost grinned at herself, thinking what cheek. She sounded as though she were an expert on the matter. She shook her head at herself in a dismissive fashion. "I believe it was someone else. If you doubt that conclusion, perhaps you would like a conversation with Carlos as well?"

Darcy looked thoroughly uncomfortable at the idea as he shifted in his seat. "I do not believe I wish to do that. It feels like an infringement upon Anne's privacy when she did not ask for my help. I shall take your word on the matter."

That caused an unexpected warmth in Lizzy's chest that spread throughout, making it difficult to breathe for a moment. She recalled the same level of trust he'd displayed in Meryton when he didn't insist on inspecting the shed of stolen property before going with her to report it to Colonel Forster and Constable Walters. There was something touching about his faith in her, at least when it came to solving mysteries.

She cleared her throat, clinging desperately to the reminder that he still disapproved of Jane and would do everything he could to block her happiness. "I have the matter well in hand."

"I shall join you this evening to be certain."

She shook her head. "I do not require your assistance, Mr. Darcy."

His lips twitched. "Indeed, but you shall have it nonetheless."

She wanted to continue to argue, but Charlotte returned then, bearing another cup and saucer and the news Maria was feeling better, though planned to sleep for the rest of the day. Lizzy declared that a wise plan and poured herself tea, determined to ignore Darcy's presence as much as politely possible, and equally determined not to reveal the drop location for the blackmailer's payment.

Of course, it might be helpful to have him along. He was a sturdy sort of fellow, and though prone to injury while allowing the villain to escape, he might prove useful. If that meant spending more time with him, she wasn't certain she could stomach the prospect. Being in the vicinity of Darcy left her feeling uneasy, with her skin itchy and too tight. Her heart was prone to race dreadfully fast at the least provocation.

She couldn't explain her reaction to him, and it seemed wiser to steer clear of him entirely. She was resolved to do just that as she drank tea, made gracious conversation, and mentally ticked down the minutes until Darcy had made a polite showing of his visit and could excuse himself without offense. When he finally left, she breathed a deep sigh of relief and leaned back in her chair.

"I do believe he fancies you, Eliza," said Charlotte.

Lizzy scoffed. "Mr. Darcy could never find anything about me of which he approves. He would never allow himself to pursue such a course of folly. Besides, I cannot stand the man."

Charlotte arched a brow. "If you insist, then it must be true." There was only the faintest note of doubt in her friend's tone, but her eyes sparkled teasingly. "You would never be one to delude yourself about your feelings for someone, of that I have no doubt."

Lizzy frowned at her. "Were I to be silly enough to have affection for Mr. Darcy, I would admit it to myself and do my best to stamp out such a weakness. I assure you I do not." She fanned herself again briskly. "The idea of Mr. Darcy courting me is quite ridiculous, I assure you."

Mr. Collins entered the room then, revealing he must've heard part of their conversation. "Indeed it is, Cousin Eliza. I am glad you are wise enough to know that and nip such girlish fantasies in the bud. After all, Mr. Darcy is practically betrothed to Miss Anne. He would never condescend to look upon you in such a favorable fashion, for you are too beneath his notice."

Lizzy heaved a sigh. "I must agree with you on that, Mr. Collins. Mr. Darcy would never consider me someone of interest or an equal. To be honest, I find that nothing but a relief."

"Indeed, it would be far beneath the man. I could hardly imagine him having the magnanimity to do such a thing. It boggles the mind, and Lady Catherine's response would be outrageous." The clergyman trembled, his fear obvious.

"I would not wish to be you if Mr. Darcy did have a *tendre* for you, for it would enrage her ladyship dreadfully so. She is determined to see Anne wed to her sister's son. I find it quite appalling you would even slightly consider the notion, Cousin Eliza."

She barely stifled the urge to roll her eyes. "I was not considering the matter, I assure you, Mr. Collins." She could have pointed out Charlotte was the one who'd made the suggestion, but she didn't want her dear friend to have to endure a long lecture either. "I wonder what Lady Catherine would think of Darcy's intentions toward Caroline Bingley?" she asked before she could think better of it. Realizing she had introduced a delicate topic, and not wishing to be a gossip, particularly in front of Mr. Collins, she quickly clamped her lips tightly closed.

Mr. Collins frowned. "Of what do you speak?"

Lizzy hesitated before shrugging a shoulder. "I am certain it is nothing. There was a brief rumor during their visit at Meryton that perhaps he planned to offer for Miss Bingley. Surely, it must have been idle gossip if he is determined to marry Miss Anne." Why that thought made it difficult to breathe, she refused to consider.

Instead, she gulped her tea, swallowing the lump in her throat that felt like it lodged in her chest, and managed to take a deep, if shaky, breath. "It matters not to me whom Mr. Darcy marries. I venture, I could not care less about the topic if I endeavored with every fiber of my being to do so."

"A wise perspective," said Mr. Collins. He still appeared disapproving as he looked at her and clicked his tongue. "I expect better than girlhood fantasies from a sensible woman like yourself, Cousin Eliza. You must not allow yourself to deviate from a logical course. I have no doubt there is a man who will take you, though he is unlikely to be a vicar and certainly not someone of Mr. Darcy's caliber. Perhaps a tradesman, or even an apprentice? I am certain we must know someone who would be an ideal match for you. What do you think, my dear?"

Charlotte stirred herself to answer in a bland fashion, saying, "I do not believe I know anyone who would suit Lizzy as well as Mr. Darcy."

Mr. Collins gasped at the suggestion. "You must be teasing me, dear Charlotte, for you are far too sensible to promote such a disparate match. It would be too far beneath Mr. Darcy to even consider such a thing."

"Indeed," and Lizzy, attempting to hide her amusement. "It would be like asking him to bend over and scrape dirt from his shoes, dear Charlotte. His valet would surely be a better choice for that task. In fact, I have no doubt his valet would be much more appropriate to woo me than Mr. Darcy."

Mr. Collins frowned again, apparently incapable of recognizing any sarcasm. "That is an admirable idea, but he is in service. Surely, he would have to leave service to get married, for how could he devote himself to his master's needs if he had a wife to balance? If you are particularly interested in Mr. Darcy's valet, perhaps we could arrange something with Mr. Darcy though? He might be willing to give the man a settlement and allow him to take up residence somewhere, perhaps a small cottage at Longbourn. I have no objection to you and your husband living there after we have taken over the land upon your father's death."

Lizzy lost all taste for amusement or sarcasm. Instead, she kept her expression neutral when she said, "I do not know Mr. Darcy's valet. If you shall excuse me, I believe I might lie down. I feel a headache coming on." Its arrival had coincided with Mr. Collins joining them, and Charlotte's sympathetic look suggested she understood that.

She marveled at her friend's patience and ability to stay married to the man while maintaining some semblance of contentment. Charlotte was certainly a strong woman, and Lizzy admired her for being able to endure the cross she bore as she left the sitting room and made her way to the small guestroom assigned to her.

THE HEADACHE SHE HAD invented, which had become slightly real though soon dissipated after being out of Mr. Collins's vicinity, provided a handy cover for her to take dinner in her room, and then she dressed in a dark gown and dark veil as she waited for the hours to tick by until midnight. When it was near time for the blackmailer's meeting, she got to her feet and slipped from her room.

She moved quietly down the hall, pausing to ensure she heard snoring, or at least silence. Maria seemed deeply asleep, with occasional snores emitting from her room. She could hear nothing coming from the Collinses' room, but she assumed they were both asleep. Charlotte had likely gone to bed a couple of hours ago, since she found it trying to maintain her energy levels all day without frequent naps and a lot of sleep at night. Mr. Collins had no doubt joined her by now, as Lizzy had observed during her stay on this occasion and others, he was typically in bed by eleven on nights they were not dining with Lady de Bourgh.

That cleared the way for her, so she slipped out the front door a few minutes later, crossing the grounds of Rosings Park with a single candle she had lit and brought with her. She had every intention of snuffing it out once she reached her destination, and she realized as she walked toward the rose garden, there might be a flaw in her plan.

She should have made the walk this morning or this afternoon in the light, to be sure she went to the right section. After all, Rosings Park had multiple rose gardens, but she hadn't considered it might be difficult to find the ornate bench mentioned in the first letter.

Now, as she stumbled through the second rose garden, finding more ornate furniture, though she wasn't certain any could be described as a bench, she started to get frustrated. Time was ticking away, and if she chose the wrong stakeout point, the blackmailer would get the payment and escape.

She should have asked Anne which garden the extortionist referenced when she told her to leave the payment. Lizzy's confidence in her investigation skills started to plummet as she realized she had no idea which garden to go to.

She nearly jumped out of her skin and let out a startled shriek before a hand closed over her mouth. It was a familiar hand, and the man smelled like Mr. Darcy, so she wasn't terribly shocked to discover it was him when she recovered from the start and stepped away as his hand lowered. "What are you doing here?"

"I am taking you to the right garden." If he was smug at all, he didn't reveal it. He simply sounded businesslike when he said, "You want the south garden. The bench mentioned is a particular favorite of my aunt's, since Uncle Lewis had it made for her shortly before his passing. Shall we?" He held out his arm, as though they were about to take a pleasant morning stroll across Rosings Park rather than hide and apprehend the blackmailer.

Surprised by the surreal turn of events, Lizzy put her arm through his. "How do you know the location?"

"I had occasion to read the entire letter over your shoulder. I suspect that must have been an older letter? This is not the first time, is it?"

She was startled by his perception, but she nodded as they walked. "This is the second such letter in two months, per Anne. The first promised to maintain discretion with the one payment, but apparently, our blackmailer is greedy."

"From my understanding, that is the way of all blackmailers, is it not? They slowly bleed their victims rather than draining them dry in one strike."

Lizzy shrugged. "I cannot say for certain, for I have never been extorted. How about you, Mr. Darcy?" she asked in a saccharine tone.

"I have done nothing worthy of blackmail, Miss Bennet." He sounded amused rather than offended by the question.

Lizzy started to say something more, but Darcy put his finger to his lips and said quietly, "We must be quiet from here. There are not many places to hide, and he will surely come soon."

She nodded her understanding while she snuffed out the candle, and they took a position near an arbor covered with roses. It provided some cover from the viewpoint of the bench but would still allow them a close enough glimpse that they could hopefully identify the man who was blackmailing Anne.

Mr. Darcy had had the good sense to dress in black too, so they blended in well with the scenery, especially since they weren't exchanging any words. Though they weren't speaking, Lizzy was hyperaware of his presence behind her, his arm brushing against hers. All she had to do was take a step back and to the right, and she could be leaning against him.

It was a strange thought, and she had no idea from where it had emerged as she struggled to stifle the idea. It had to be because of that vexing kiss he had thrust upon her. She couldn't deny part of it had been a pleasurable experience, but that it came from Fitzwilliam Darcy was something she could hardly bear. She could only explain the moment as insanity brought about by their shared anger.

Though he had been the one to instigate the kiss, she couldn't pretend she had tried to push him away. In fact, for a moment, she'd eagerly pulled him forward until regaining control and stepping back. She shook her head now at the thought, wondering that she could have behaved so wantonly and surprised she'd managed to stifle deep thought about it until now.

It was an unfortunate time to be dissecting the situation, and she tried to bring herself back to the present, focusing on the need to identify the blackmailer. If only he weren't so blasted close, with his scent permeating her, wrapping around her in a comfortable fashion that was both soothing and aggravating in a way she couldn't explain.

Realizing she was thinking about him again, and struggling to recall the taste of his mouth, she shook her head at her silliness. This distraction wouldn't do.

He put a hand on her shoulder and squeezed gently, as though asking about her health. Perhaps he'd seen the wild headshaking and thought she was ill. She could hardly fault him for that assumption, and she resolved to keep herself still.

They didn't have to wait long, which helped the task of keeping her mind from Darcy and that shocking kiss. Mr. Collins appeared in front of them moments later. Lizzy couldn't see his face, but she recognized his form, not to mention his familiar tricorn hat that was out of style.

She felt a little disappointment that he would do such a thing, but she wasn't terribly surprised. The shipment of marble and orders of expensive tea from India suddenly made a lot more sense, and she doubted they were gifts bestowed by Lady Catherine. More likely, they were tributes paid by Miss Anne to keep her secret.

Darcy stiffened, clearly intent on approaching Mr. Collins, and Lizzy put her hand on his chest to stop him. He froze and looked down at her when she shook her head. She didn't speak until Mr. Collins had retrieved the small packet wrapped in oilskin and stuffed it into his coat before slinking off. Once he was out of hearing range, she said, "I believe we should confront him tomorrow in the light of day."

"I have half a mind to deal with him right now." There was a fierce anger about Darcy, revealing just how protective he was of Anne. For the first time, Lizzy wondered if he actually planned to marry his cousin, but she couldn't reconcile that with his plans to ask for Caroline Bingley.

More likely, he just cared for Anne, who he seemed to regard more like a sister than a potential fiancée. She was relieved by that, but there was no relief for knowing he was going to marry Caroline Bingley.

She refused to wonder why it bothered her to imagine him marrying someone. She told herself it was simply because it was Caroline Bingley, and she would feel pity for any man who intended to tether himself to that woman. There was nothing more to it, and certainly nothing related to that impetuous kiss. She refused to contemplate otherwise.

After a moment, his shoulders sagged slightly, and he loosened his stiff posture. "I shall defer to your suggestion, but we will be speaking to him tomorrow. This cannot stand."

Lizzy nodded frantically. "I quite agree, Mr. Darcy."

"I shall escort you back to the rectory." When Lizzy opened her mouth to object, he sent her a warning glance. "Do not argue with me about this, Miss Bennet. I will be sure you return safely to Hunsford Rectory, or you can sleep at Rosings Park. I am certain you would like to make an explanation for that in the morning?"

She glared at him, but she submitted to his chivalrous instincts, though it was wrapped in the implied threat. "Very well, Mr. Darcy. I am quite capable of walking across the grounds by myself, but if you insist, you may accompany me."

"Nothing would give me more pleasure," he said in a tone filled with rancor.

Lizzy almost snorted and then giggled at the juxtaposition of his words versus his tone. Knowing he was doing so grudgingly allowed her to accept his gallant offer, and she put her arm through his again as they walked across Rosings Park and back to the rectory. She was inside and in her room moments later, doing her best to focus on the outcome of the investigation and not think at all about Mr. Darcy's kiss, or their interactions since.

Chapter Seven

Fitzwilliam wanted to show up at the rectory the moment he woke, but he knew he had to wait for a better time. He spent the day pacing and distracting himself with conversation first with Richard, and then with Anne. He found her in the music room, but she sat in front of the harp without playing it.

As he drew nearer, she stirred herself and looked at him. She gave him a smile, but she was clearly uneasy. No doubt, she was still consumed with worry about the person blackmailing her.

Darcy stood near the chair beside her. "May I sit down?" At her nod, he took it and turned the chair to face her. "I must speak with you bluntly, Anne."

Her shoulders went back, and she seemed to be bracing herself. "Yes, Fitzwilliam?"

"I know about the situation."

She scowled, and then she looked angry. "Did Miss Bennet reveal it to you? I thought I had her utmost discretion."

He lifted a hand, compelled to defend Lizzy both because it was the right thing to do, and for reasons he couldn't quite express. "I came upon her as she was reading the letter out on the grounds, and I confess, I saw the contents over her shoulder. She did not reveal to me who the victim was. It was my own observations that allowed me to guess. As it were, we watched for the blackmailer last night, and we have identified him."

Her mouth dropped open, and she gasped. "Will he ruin me, Fitzwilliam?"

He straightened his shoulders in a determined fashion. "I do not believe he will have the chance. He is in a precarious position, and I intend to remind him of that when I confront him today. Your troubles should be over with the man."

"Who is it?" asked Anne. Her lips trembled for a moment. "It is not Carlos, is it?" She seemed weak as she asked the question.

He reached out and squeezed her hand in a restful fashion. "It is not. Once the matter is resolved, I will reveal everything to you, or I shall allow Miss Bennet to do so. I simply wanted to put your mind at ease."

She nodded, and then bit her lip. "You are not going to tell Mama?"

He shook his head. "It is not my place to tell her. I do wish you could find a way that did not require sneaking around and putting yourself at risk, but I also understand why you are reluctant to confide in Aunt Catherine. She is likely to take the news poorly."

Anne giggled then, a carefree sound likely generated by relief. "That is undeniably an understatement."

After having lunch with Anne and Richard, since Lady Catherine had chosen to take a tray in her room, he went for a walk around Rosings Park. When finally enough time had passed, he headed toward Hunsford Rectory, intent on confronting Collins and ending his extortion campaign against his cousin.

Miss Charlotte appeared surprised to see him back for a second day in a row, but there was definitely a hint of interest in her gaze as she made a show of leaving Lizzy and Fitzwilliam alone for a short time to ensure the housekeeper was brewing the right blend of tea for the day. As soon as they were alone, he moved from the chair to sit beside her on the settee so they could have a more intimate conversation. "How do you propose to do this?"

"I have given the matter consideration, and I think we should approach him together. He is in his garden, so after we have tea with

Charlotte, perhaps I can suggest showing you Mr. Collins's new marble, and we could take a walk there?"

He nodded. "I intend to be harsh with the man." He said that as a warning to her, wanting her to prepare herself. "I will have no mercy."

Lizzy nodded, and she didn't seem bothered by that, though she did say, "Please remember he knows Miss Anne's secret though. We are in the superior position, but he has a level of power."

He was grim as he acknowledged that with a nod. "I shall be disabusing him of that belief, I assure you, Lizzy."

She stiffened slightly at the use of her sobriquet, but she didn't rebuke him. Instead, she gave him a small smile. "It seems whenever we are together, some type of crime must follow. We simply have to stop meeting this way, Mr. Darcy."

He let his lips relax into a slight smile, though his shoulders remained stiff with tension at the forthcoming confrontation. "I do believe that would not be nearly as much fun, though I suppose it is the safer course of action."

"It is quite fun to undertake the challenge of solving mysteries," said Lizzy with a hint of surprise in her voice. "I did not expect to enjoy such a thing, or to have some skill for it. It is hardly a ladylike achievement though. It is nothing akin to knowing all the modern languages and being able to sketch every impression before me."

He flushed, suspecting she was poking some fun at him over the conversation they'd had in Netherfield's library with Miss Bingley, where Lizzy had expressed her doubt that any woman could exist who might match all of Fitzwilliam's exacting standards. He had the crazy impulse to tell her he had met just such a woman, but he kept the impulse in check. He was no less committed to the course of action he'd chosen earlier, before mistakenly believing she was being blackmailed and getting sidetracked, but they had to deal with this unpleasant business first.

Charlotte returned then, and they enjoyed a cup of tea, though he was antsy and trying his best not to appear impatient. When he finished a second tea cake, Lizzy set aside her cup and saucer and said, "Mr. Collins has had a marvelous shipment of marble straight from Italy. He is using it to make a walkway in his garden. Would you like to see it, Mr. Darcy?"

He feigned an interest. "Italian marble does sound delightful. I would be happy for you to escort me." Realizing it would be rude not to invite Charlotte, he said, "Will you join us, Mrs. Collins?"

Charlotte reacted in the way he'd hoped. She laughed and waved a hand. "No, but please go ahead. I have heard enough about the marble in the preceding days, and it is about time for my afternoon nap. I hope you find it as enthralling as Mr. Collins. He does talk incessantly about it." There was a note of affectionate endurance in her tone as she said that.

Darcy stood up, waiting for Lizzy to get to her feet and then Charlotte. They stood as Charlotte walked out of the sitting room, and Mrs. Tesch came to retrieve the tray before they left the house and walked around the back to the garden, where Mr. Collins was seriously working.

Being the soft sort of man he was, Fitzwilliam was surprised to see he was doing most of the work himself. Perhaps he wanted to make the blackmail funds stretch as far as possible. The thought filled him with cold anger.

Chapter Eight

Lizzy could feel Mr. Darcy stiffening beside her, and without thought, she reached out and squeezed his hand in a comforting fashion, hoping to distract him from the surge of anger she could feel seething in him. Almost as soon as she touched him, she immediately let go. Though she'd been wearing a glove, as had he, she swore she could feel his skin against her own, and it left her unsettled as they approached Mr. Collins.

He was on his knees, but as they got closer, he lumbered to his feet and lifted a hand in greeting. "Mr. Darcy, how delightful to see you. Have you come to admire the marble?"

"I have come to see what my cousin's funds paid for," said Darcy in a cold tone.

Lizzy almost grinned at the way Mr. Collins paled. "The... Pardon?"

"You can drop all pretense, Mr. Collins. We know you have been blackmailing poor Miss Anne," said Lizzy, making her voice thick with shame. "I am appalled a relative of mine could behave in such a fashion."

Mr. Collins reached into his pocket for a handkerchief and used it to wipe his brow, which was suddenly sweating copiously. "I do not know what you are talking about, Cousin Eliza."

Darcy loomed closer. "We saw you last night, Mr. Collins. My cousin confided in Lizzy, and Lizzy offered to help her find the person extorting her. We recognized you when you picked up the money. I am certain if I search the rectory, I will find at least the oilskin, and likely some of the banknotes remaining. Surely, you have not had time to spend them all yet?"

Mr. Collins started to tremble, and he wiped ineffectually at his face as sweat poured off him. "You do not understand, Mr. Darcy. She is engaged with the groom. The groom! It is shameful business, and she is to be your wife. Should you not be dealing with the matter of Anne's treachery rather than my asking for a token to maintain silence?"

"The amount you requested both times is hardly a token," said Lizzy in a scolding voice. "You have caused the lady much grief as she struggled to figure out how she could meet your demands on a continuing basis. You must know this will end now, Mr. Collins. If I hear from Miss Anne that you are continuing demands for payment, I will tell Charlotte, and I will also reveal the news to everyone in Meryton. When you become the proprietor of Longbourn, I assure you it will be a most uncomfortable experience for you if everyone in the community knows the cut of your character."

He trembled again, looking like he might weep. "Please do not do that, Cousin. I simply wanted some creature comforts. The salary of a vicar does not go far enough to cover those things."

"So you would blackmail a helpless young woman to see to your comforts?" Darcy sounded furious. "I should destroy you right now, Collins. All it would take is revealing to my aunt your actions, and she would withdraw her patronage."

Mr. Collins's spine stiffened. "That would require revealing Miss Anne's betrayal of your betrothal, Mr. Darcy. I cannot imagine you would be eager to do such a thing."

With a grunt, Fitzwilliam stepped closer, grasping Mr. Collins by the front of his shirt. "I tell you now, I will not be blackmailed, and I will not allow it to continue for Anne. She is not and never has been my fiancée. Nor will she ever be."

"Mr. Darcy is about to become engaged to Miss Bingley," said Lizzy. "Whatever Lady de Bourgh wishes to happen will not be occurring, and you will not use that as a tool of negotiation. You will cease all blackmail attempts immediately."

Darcy stiffened at her words, and he shot her a surprised look before returning his attention to Mr. Collins. "I assure you, if I have to reveal the situation, I will. I can help protect Anne from Lady Catherine's anger, but I would do nothing to shield you. You shall be out of the rectory and in disgrace. You will find it impossible to find another position, and you will have to scrape by a living until the day Mr. Bennet passes away. In that time, I shall dedicate myself to ensuring his continued good health and long life. I will also assist him by hiring a team of solicitors who might help him challenge the entailment."

"B...but Charlotte, and the baby? What about them?"

Darcy glared at him. "They should not be my concern, but I would never allow them to suffer. I cannot imagine Mrs. Collins is so attached to you that she would refuse the offer of a small cottage at Pemberley to be free of you, Mr. Collins."

Even as Mr. Collins trembled under the force of his cold anger, a surge of admiration went through Lizzy. She'd had threats to offer as well, and while she could've made his life uncomfortable, Darcy had the power to truly destroy it. She couldn't help admiring that.

"I promise I shall not mention the subject to Miss Anne again. I do not need to return the money, do I? I have expenses."

Lizzy was disgusted by Mr. Collins, and Darcy appeared to be the same, but he released his hold and shoved the man back lightly, putting distance between them without causing Mr. Collins to fall to the ground.

"You may keep the payments you have collected, but they are the only ones. Do you understand me, Mr. Collins? From this day forward, it will slip your mind completely that Anne has found happiness with someone you consider beneath her. I assure you, if and when the relationship is revealed, she will have my full support to be with her groom, and anyone who stands in her way would not like to feel my wrath. Are we agreed?"

"Yes, Mr. Darcy." The man was still sniveling and trembling, but he seemed to be properly cowed.

Apparently, Darcy couldn't stand more interaction with him, because he turned and walked away. Lizzy planned to return to the rectory, but as she started to do so, his hand clamped around her wrist, and he said, "Walk with me." There was a commanding note in his voice that was difficult to resist, and Lizzy was disconcerted to realize she didn't want to.

Telling herself she simply wanted to have a postmortem discussion about the confrontation with Mr. Collins, to ensure they hadn't overlooked anything, she fell into step with him. Yes, this was strictly about the extortion business and nothing else.

They walked a while before he spoke, and she realized they were far away from the rectory, and not close to Lady Catherine's home either. It was just the two of them, and they were virtually alone, though they were in an exposed field. She felt no alarm for that. "You handled him masterfully, Mr. Darcy." She couldn't keep the admiration from her tone.

He looked at her in surprise, his gaze narrowing. "I confess, I am expecting you to follow that with something to thoroughly diminish me."

She grinned. "In this case, I have nothing to criticize. I had a plan, and though I think my threats might've held some weight with him, I fear if he got greedy enough or wanted something badly enough, he would still give in to his baser urges, assuming either I would not follow through with my threats, or gossip about him being a blackmailer would die down before he took over Longbourn. I concede you having more power over him and the situation is quite useful, and I thank you for your interference."

He snorted. "There is the insult I was expecting. I am pleased you appreciate me inserting myself into *your* investigation," he said with only a faint hint of mocking. "I do have more leverage over the man."

"Did you mean it?" asked Lizzy hesitantly.

He frowned. "Mean what?"

"When you told Mr. Collins you would support Miss Anne if she decides to go public with her relationship with Carlos? Were you just telling him that to intimidate him, or did you mean it?"

He scowled. "Of course, I meant it. I do not say things I do not mean, Miss Bennet."

She was bereft that he was back to using Miss Bennet instead of Lizzy for reasons she couldn't explain. It had been a momentary lapse of propriety, likely engendered by their cooperation to find the blackmailer, but she wished they could maintain that level of informality, which disconcerted her.

"I know you have no plans to marry her, but I wanted to be sure you would still truly support her. It is a scandalous thought, and I can imagine Society will revile her for a long time to come if she marries her groom."

He nodded, his lips pursing in disapproval. "Society is quick to make judgments, but they do not always understand the reasons behind someone making the choices they do."

"Is that why you are marrying Miss Bingley?" asked Lizzy with audacity she hadn't known she had. It should've been a verboten topic, but she couldn't deny she was curious about his reasons. Only curious, of course. She felt nothing else, but she couldn't imagine why he had chosen to ask for Caroline Bingley. She didn't seem like the kind of woman who would make him happy long-term.

He scowled at her. "Where did you get the impression I am about to marry Caroline Bingley?"

Lizzy put her hands on her hips as she frowned up at him. "You said it yourself at the Netherfield ball."

His eyebrow attempted to recede into his hairline. "I did?" He sounded shocked. "I am certain I would remember that conversation, Miss Bennet. You must have misunderstood."

She opened her mouth to protest, but as she reviewed their conversation, she realized he'd never blatantly stated he was marrying Caroline Bingley. That was simply the impression she'd gotten from his words. "Perhaps I did. Does that mean you are not becoming betrothed to Miss Bingley?"

He appeared to try to hide it, but he couldn't completely stifle the shudder that went through him. "I would rather marry Anne than Miss Bingley, and Anne is like a sister to me. No, I most emphatically am not about to offer for Miss Bingley, nor will I ever be. That would be to her pleasure, but to my displeasure."

Lizzy nodded, unable to explain the relief sweeping through her, and then attributing it only to that she hadn't kissed a man who was about to be engaged. That would've been an unforgivable action.

"I confess, my thoughts have turned to matrimony of late," said Darcy unexpectedly.

Lizzy cocked her head slightly, her stomach clenching at the words. She had no right to be bothered by the fact Mr. Darcy was contemplating marriage. Of course, he was. A man like him must be in want of a wife, and she would likely be a paragon of virtue and the pinnacle of Society. "I suppose it is time for you to consider the matter, being six-and-twenty."

He nodded absently. "There are men in my family who have married much later, so it is not a matter of age. Rather, it is a matter of finding someone with whom I have a mutual accord. I believe I have found such a person."

Lizzy frowned, wishing she could excuse herself from the conversation. Deciding she could, she said, "I must return to the rectory now, but thank you for your help, Mr. Darcy. Will you relay the news to Anne, or shall I?"

"Perhaps you could write her a vague letter, but I will speak with her more directly."

She nodded and took a step back. "That sounds like a good plan. I shall see you later."

"Lizzy," he said softly.

She froze before slowly turning back to face him. "Yes, Mr. Darcy?" She was a stickler for using his last name, though part of her wanted to yield and use Fitzwilliam. She wanted to hear how it sounded on her tongue just once when uttered in an intimate fashion, though she had no right to do so. After all, he was talking about getting married to someone, and he obviously had a candidate in mind.

"You must allow me to confess my ardent affection for you, Lizzy. I understand your family is a terrible burden, and your mother in particular is a trial, but I am prepared to stand fast against that. I will weather the gossip that comes from lowering my standards and station to marry someone with your status. While you lack certain accomplishments, and I suspect it might be a difficult adjustment for you to go from Longbourn to the Mistress of Pemberley, I will be patient as I guide you through it. You have enough to recommend you that I am able to overlook your flaws. Will you do me the honor of being my wife?"

Lizzy stared at him, mouth open, and utterly aghast. "You are asking me to marry you?"

He nodded at her, looking like a benevolent god bestowing a favor on an acolyte.

It took everything she had not to laugh. She was afraid if she did, she would either dissolve into screaming, or she might start crying. "No, thank you, Mr. Darcy."

He frowned. "You are refusing?"

She licked her lips. "I must."

He reached out a hand as though to touch her before dropping it at his side. "I appreciate you trying to be noble, but do not deny yourself this opportunity. I am willingly lowering myself, and I do not expect you to reject me to try to save me. I genuinely wish to take you as my wife."

"I cannot imagine why with all my shortcomings, Mr. Darcy. How is it you are able to overlook them all?" she asked too sweetly.

Either he was too self-absorbed in general, or just oblivious at the moment, because he seemed to take her question at face value. "I admit, there are many things that detract, but I have come to admire a great many other qualities about you, Lizzy. You have a quick and lively mind, and I am certain we shall not grow bored with each other. It is an important ingredient for a successful marriage. There is clear passion between us, as I am sure you must concede after the kiss we shared."

She grudgingly nodded, unable to deny that.

"You have a good nature, and you are quick to defend those weaker than you. These are all admirable traits, and I feel I can overcome any of the negatives to accentuate your positives. "

"Most gracious of you," she said dryly. "I must still decline."

He looked thunderstruck, and his brows gradually drew together as his shock turned to a frown. "Is that the only reply I am to receive, or will you explain why?"

"It is the politest one I can give you, Mr. Darcy," she said coolly.

He took a step closer. "Dispense with politeness and be honest. Why will you not accept my offer?"

"How could I when you have made it so grudgingly, and with such clear reluctance? Perhaps you do love me, but it is something that is causing you great pain. I have no doubt it will pass soon enough, like a bout of indigestion. I could never burden you with all my negatives, Mr. Darcy, for I deserve better."

His eyes widened, and his lips tightened. "You deserve better than me?"

"Indeed, I do. I deserve a man who treats me as an equal and does not weigh my assets against my losses to determine if I am worth the effort to love. Furthermore, I could never marry a man who would deliberately meddle in the relationship between my sister and the man she loves. You would break my heart as surely as you break my sister's if I compromised myself to lower my standards to do so. You are too proud and cold for me, and I suspect this is an aberration from which you will soon recover."

"I am exactly the man I was raised to be. I have standards that are rigorous, and I take pride in that. You make it sound like a flaw."

She shrugged a shoulder. "It does seem like a flaw when amplified through you, Mr. Darcy. I have no doubt you can be quite a decent human being, but I am not the woman to bring out that side of you. That much is obvious. You stand too much in the way of happiness for others for me to ever contemplate being happy with you. So again, I thank you for your proposal, but I fervently decline."

He nodded stiffly at her. "In that case, I shall bid you good day."

"Goodbye, Mr. Darcy."

He nodded at her once more but didn't reciprocate as he stormed across the field, heading toward Rosings Park. After a moment, Lizzy turned in the direction of the rectory to make her way back. There was a heavy ache in her chest she couldn't explain, though she might've labeled it at least a bruised heart.

Part of her had affection for Mr. Darcy, at least the gentler sides she'd seen at various moments, but there was still too much of the prideful aristocrat in him for her to ever seriously contemplate the idea of marriage to the man. If she gave in to the impulse, they would both be sorry. Inevitably, he would quickly come to his senses and realize the mistake he had made, and he would be trapped in a miserable marriage.

She had no doubt she would be miserable as well, because he would always be seeking to change her into something she wasn't, and he would never relent on his disapproval of Jane and Mr. Bingley's relationship. As long as he was determined to thwart her sister's heart, Lizzy could not risk entrusting her own to him.

She returned to the rectory a short time later and found Charlotte in the sitting room. She did her best to clear her thoughts as she sat down with her friend. "I thought you were going to take a nap?"

Charlotte nodded. "I planned to, but Mr. Collins came in and looked quite upset. He said he was feeling ill, so I allowed him the bedroom to lie down. You look like you are also feeling unwell, Lizzy. You did not eat any of the fish Maria had, did you?"

Lizzy burst into laughter, though it had a slightly hysterical edge. "I am not sick from fish, but from unwanted love."

Charlotte frowned as she came to sit beside her. "I do not understand."

Amid her bitter laughter, Lizzy managed to convey the gist of Mr. Darcy's proposal. "Can you imagine?" she finished moments later. "It was so insulting, and then he seemed shocked I was not eager to accept."

Charlotte, with a tender heart like Jane, seemed more appalled than amused. "What a wretched proposal. The man lacks social graces, and that is inexcusable."

Lizzy laughed again. "You must admit it is funny."

Charlotte's lips pursed in disapproval. "I do not think so. I find it tragic."

Lizzy frowned. "How so?"

"The man clearly loves you, but he bungled all attempts to relay the strength of his emotions. Surely, he must be deriding himself even now for how poorly he worded his offer. Perhaps he will make another attempt, and you will find it more pleasing."

"How can I find it pleasing when I know the man, and how he is? He deliberately stands between Jane and Mr. Bingley, and he loves me with utmost reluctance. Can you imagine the next proposal? He is likely to try to bribe me with a trinket or point out all the financial benefits for marrying a man like him. He would never approach me in a straight and honest fashion, speaking of emotion on a level we both share." Lizzy started to giggle again as she imagined the next proposal he might utter, building it up to be utterly ridiculous in her mind until she was practically hysterical with laughter.

Charlotte looked disapproving, but she didn't try to stop her. She didn't seem at all surprised when Lizzy's laughter suddenly turned to tears as she started sobbing. Instead, Charlotte took her into her arms and held her without judgment. Lizzy appreciated the comfort of her friend's embrace as she cried tears she wasn't entirely sure why she was shedding. Or perhaps she knew, but she didn't want to look closer and discover for certain.

Chapter Nine

Darcy returned to Rosings Park in a fit of anger, taking only a few moments to dispatch a note for Lady Catherine, and then another for his cousin to assure her the situation was handled. After that, he tasked his valet with packing his things, and he was in the process of leaving his room when Richard came in.

"What is all this?" asked his cousin.

He spared a brief glance for the colonel. "I am departing for London. I find I can no longer stay at Rosings Park. I have lost all stomach for the task, and duty be hanged."

Richard looked sympathetic. "I did notice Aunt Catherine was rather forcefully pushing the idea of you formally offering for Anne this time. I am sorry, old chap. It must be quite vexing."

Darcy was content to let him think that was the reason he was leaving. He had no interest in sharing his humiliation or revealing how disdainful Elizabeth Bennet had been when he asked to marry her. He still burned with outrage at the gall of her reaction.

She had laughed at him, insulted him, and implied he was beneath her. The very nerve of the woman. What could he possibly see in her, and how had he convinced himself he wanted to marry her? It was baffling now that he thought about it. He must've simply given in to a moment of insanity, and he should thank her instead of being angry. After all, she'd saved him from himself, but she had done it in a cold and condescending fashion that still chafed him.

"You are off to London?"

"I am. The season will soon be underway, and Georgiana plans to join me there. I do hope I shall see you in London."

"I have some leave coming around Christmas, so perhaps I can get away to join you then. I must return to my regiment after my visit here at Rosings Park." Richard came forward and gave him a hug. "Until we meet again, Darcy."

"Until then, Fitzie." Darcy intended to be a different version of himself then. He was determined to eradicate this irrational love for Elizabeth Bennet. She clearly had no use for it and had rejected it soundly, so it was in his best interest to make sure he carved it out and thoroughly excised any remnants of it.

He was unlikely to see her in London, and once he returned to Pemberley, he would have no reason to visit her area of the country again. If Bingley stood fast, he would let go of his tenancy at the end of his lease, and they could both set the chapter of the Bennet girls behind them, writing it off as deplorable mistakes they had nearly made, and consoling themselves at some point in the future for their lucky escape.

Yes, he should be grateful for Lizzy having a clearer head than he had. Clinging to that, he departed Rosings Park less than an hour later, having slipped out without needing to confront Lady Catherine, and he didn't see Lizzy again. As his carriage took him past the rectory at Hunsford Park, he determinedly kept his eyes focused ahead, refusing to glance and hope for even a glimpse of her. If he never saw Miss Bennet again, that would be for the best.

This series needs to be read in order, just like Jane Austen's masterpiece.
The series in order:
Rapacity & Rancor[1]
Abduction & Acrimony[2]

---

1. https://books2read.com/u/4ApM1d

---

2. https://books2read.com/u/mBwB1k

3. https://books2read.com/u/bxQGPe

4. https://books2read.com/u/bzZyAn

5. https://books2read.com/u/mddaAE

6. https://www.subscribepage.com/JAFF

About The Author

Abbey is a diehard Jane Austen fan and has loved Fitzwilliam since the first time she "met" him at age thirteen upon borrowing the book from the school library. He is the ideal man, though Abbey's husband is a close second. Abbey enjoys writing various steamy and sweet Jane Austen variations, but "Pride & Prejudice" (and Mr. Darcy) will always be her favorite.

Did you love *Extortion & Enmity: A Pride & Prejudice Variation Mystery Romance*? Then you should read *Murder & Misjudgment: A Pride & Prejudice Variation Mystery Romance*[1] by Abbey North!

A trip to London promises to be exciting as Lizzy tries to help Jane find a way to meet with Mr. Bingley. Her own experience is enlivened by meeting Lord Aumley, a handsome young viscount thrust into the world of Society unexpectedly. She wants to like Lord Aumley as more than a friend, but when she sees Darcy again, she accepts she cares more about the prideful man than she should. Her heart seems set on him, though her mind is still resisting the idea.

While making it clear to the young viscount she has no interest beyond friendship, a homicide crosses her path, followed by another soon after. When Darcy notices the victims bear an uncanny

---

1. https://books2read.com/u/bzZyAn

2. https://books2read.com/u/bzZyAn

resemblance to Lizzy, he swears to protect her—even if it means keeping her under lock and key. Lizzy isn't certain she's even at risk, but she wants to find the murderer in their midst while perhaps seeing unexpected changes in Darcy that lead her to contemplate his previous proposal with renewed attention.

This is part four of the completed five-book "Crime & Courtship" series. They are intended to be read in order and follow roughly the same timeline and locations as J.A.'s masterpiece. The first mystery takes place in Meryton. The next is at Netherfield, followed by Hunsford, then London, and finally Pemberley. The story arc continues throughout all five parts, compromising one long read broken into five sections. A mystery is central to each installment, so you could call this a cozy mystery sweet Regency romance.

While Abbey sometimes writes sensual JAFF, this series is strictly SWEET.

Also by Abbey North

A Month To Love
Reproach (Part One)
Resentment (Part Two)
Rapport (Part Three)
A Month To Love Compilation

Crime & Courtship
Rapacity & Rancor: A Pride & Prejudice Variation
Abduction & Acrimony : A Pride & Prejudice Variation Mystery
Romance
Extortion & Enmity: A Pride & Prejudice Variation Mystery
Romance
Murder & Misjudgment: A Pride & Prejudice Variation Mystery
Romance
Perfidy & Promises: A Pride & Prejudice Variation Mystery Romance
Crime & Courtship: A Sweet Pride & Prejudice Mystery Romance
Compilation

Darcy's Courtesan
Adversity (Darcy's Courtesan, Part One)

Avidity (Darcy's Courtesan, Part Two)
Amity (Darcy's Courtesan, Part Three)
Darcy's Courtesan: A Sensual "Pride & Prejudice" Variation

Marriage & Mysteries
Honeymoon & Hemlock

Mr. Darcy's Secret Stories
Mistaken Masquerade: A Pride & Prejudice Variation
Mischief & Matchmaking: A "Pride & Prejudice" Variation

Standalone
Christmas At Pemberley: A Pride & Prejudice Variation
A Scandalous Proposition: A Pride & Prejudice Variation
Shadow of Darcy: A Sensual Pride & Prejudice Paranormal Variation
Darcy's Obsession
Blackmailing Lizzy: A "Pride & Prejudice" Variation
Darcy's Wicked Game
Danger With Darcy: A Sensual "Pride & Prejudice" Variation
Passion & Prostrations: A Sensual "Pride & Prejudice" Variation
Darcy's Debt: A Sensual Pride & Prejudice Variation
Obstinacy & Obligation: A Sweet Pride & Prejudice Variation
Darcy's Alibi: A Sweet "Pride & Prejudice" Variation
Marooned With Darcy: A Sensual "Pride & Prejudice" Variation
Compromising Mr. Darcy: A Steamy "Pride & Prejudice" Variation
Marrying Mr. Darcy: A Sensual "Pride & Prejudice" Variation
Darcys' First Christmastide